MORE
FIVE-MINUTE
MYSTERIES

Ken Weber

RUNNING PRESS
PHILADELPHIA · LONDON

ISBN 1–56138–058–X

29 28 27 26 25 24 23 22 21
Digit on the right indicates the number of this printing.

Cover design by Toby Schmidt
Cover Illustration by Beth McHenry

Any resemblance of any characters to persons living or dead is purely coincidental.

Printed and bound in the United States by Command Web Offset, Secaucus, NJ.

This book may be ordered by mail from the publisher. Please add $2.50 for postage and handling.
But try your bookstore first!
Running Press Book Publishers
125 South Twenty-second Street
Philadelphia, Pennsylvania 19103-4399

To Beau,
who was there for all the words

Contents

1

A Clean Place to Make an End of It

WHAT INTRIGUED BOB GIBSON — BOTHERED him, actually — was how *clean* the inside of the car was. Someone, quite possibly the dead woman herself, had vacuumed the interior rugs with special care. There wasn't a speck of dust anywhere on the dash, either, or along the steering column; even the short stalks behind the knobs on the radio had been wiped. The leather cover over the gearshift box had been cleaned of the dust and grit that always collect in the creases. That had taken a wet cloth or a chamois, Bob realized. So the cleaning was not just a casual, spontaneous effort.

It wasn't a new car. From where he was leaning into it, with both fists pressed into the driver's seat, Bob peered a little closer at the odometer. The light wasn't all that good in the little garage, and the car had been backed in so that the waning winter daylight from the open garage door came through the windshield directly into his face. Still, he could make out the figures: 47,583. No, not a new car at all. But one in great shape.

Bob leaned across the seat and, with the tip of his index finger, ticked the switch on the armrest to lower the passenger window just a bit. He checked to see if the earnest young policeman at the door had noticed, but he hadn't. If he had, and objected, Bob would have argued. The smell in the car was nauseating, and he needed to relieve it by letting a bit of draft through.

It was a smell he'd encountered before. Not so often as to be familiar with it. Maybe a half-dozen times or so in the past thirty years, but after the first time he'd never forgotten. It was the smell of a body in the early stages of decomposition: a hint of sweet and a hint of foul. Sickening.

The smell clung, too. The garage door had been open for several hours, ever since the body had been discovered earlier, around noon. But the whole building was still filled with the odor, and Bob knew it would be a long time before the fabric in the car would be free of it.

Inside the car, of course, it was worse. The doors had been open only long enough for the photographer to do her grisly job, and then again when the coroner removed the body. Bob was here to tow away the car to the police pound.

Over his years as owner of Palgrave Motors, Bob had come to know the police very well and he was the one they invariably called in situations like this. Therefore it was not, as he had reflected only seconds before, the first time he had been called to the scene of a suicide. Nevertheless, although all he had to do was take away the car, the whole business gave him the creeps.

According to the coroner, the woman — Bob didn't know her name — had backed the car into the little garage some forty to fifty hours ago, closed the door and simply sat there with the motor running until the inevitable happened. The body had gone unnoticed for almost two days, the coroner estimated.

"You didn't touch anything, did you?"

It was Officer Shaw. Bob hadn't heard him come in. The young policeman had been left behind by the investigating detective with specific and stern instructions that nothing was to be disturbed. Shaw took the order seriously.

Bob looked at him, uncertain just how to put his suspicions. He pointed to the two-way radio in Shaw's belt.

"Can you call your sergeant on that?"

Shaw didn't answer; he just looked at Bob curiously.

"'Cause I think he'll want to take another look at all this," the older man said. "Missed something, I think."

Why has Bob Gibson drawn this conclusion?

2

Chasing the Bank Robbers

KAY FIRST HEARD THE POWERFUL engine as she topped the rise that bumped up at the crest of the long hill. Muscle car, she could tell. Trans Am probably. Or a customized pickup with all kinds of soup. Speeding, too, she knew. Well, it was going to have to slow down pretty sharply when it caught up to her, because there was a stop sign where the Twentieth Side Road met the Tenth Line in a T just ahead. In the past, more than one car had gone roaring through into the field beyond. She should know, too. Kay MacDuffee was number two in Caledon Traffic Section.

"Not today, I'm not!" Kay said out loud. Loud enough to catch the attention of the dog pacing along beside her. His tongue was lolling out after the walk up the big hill.

"Today I'm on vacation," she said, patting the head of the big red setter. "Sorry. *We're* on vacation. Right, old pal? And we don't care how fast they're blasting up the hill. It's not our problem. Today, anyway!"

The car was fast, all right. It whooshed past her with a

4

tremendous ululation from the decelerating engine, signal light blinking, then brake lights flashing in a cloud of choking exhaust. It didn't stop at the sign but slid into a bit of a fishtail as it turned left and tore hard up the Tenth.

It *was* a Trans Am. Black. License...

Kay gritted her teeth.

"I'm on vacation!" she shouted, and willed herself not to see the license number.

The shout was drowned in an engine clatter she hadn't even heard; it came so close upon the heels of the first car. Another Trans Am! Just as noisy and, if anything, faster than the first!

Kay braced herself for the whoosh and the foulness of the exhaust of this second one. She was an inveterate walker — the steep long hill at the end of the Twentieth was a favorite route — and she knew muscle cars not only sounded uncivilized, they smelled worse.

This one fishtailed even more than the first as it hit the gravel, for the Tenth was not paved to the south. Like the first car it was black, and it had roared to the corner with brake lights flashing, although this driver didn't bother with signals.

The roar of the two cars gradually fading in opposite directions accentuated the silence that began to gather around Kay once more. She shook her head. One thing she liked about her vacation time was that she could walk after nine in the morning when the traffic was almost nonexistent. Nothing quiet about today!

She crossed the road at the stop sign to walk back down the hill on the other side. Then she heard the third car and, almost immediately, saw it pop over the rise. The red light was flashing. No siren, though. It screeched to a stop beside her as the policeman in the passenger seat rolled down his window.

"Pardon me, ma'am. We... Sergeant MacDuffee! What... oh yeah, you live out here, don't you? Listen. This is heavy. National Trust was held up back in town about ten, fifteen minutes ago. We just got the call. Getaway's a black Trans Am. The license has a seven and a five. Don't have anything more except they had to be local. Car disappeared in a subdivision, seemed to know exactly where to go, then apparently headed this way. A lady in her garden back at the Eighth says she's sure she saw a black car tear up this way only a minute ago. You see it?"

"Have you got a backup?" Kay asked.

"No. We're alone."

"Darn."

Kay MacDuffee has to send the patrol car after one of the two Trans Ams. Which is her most likely choice?

3

The Power
of Chance

AFTER THIRTY-SEVEN YEARS ON the bench, Tom Houghton
had developed a pretty dim view of the role of chance in human
affairs. He was by nature a logical person, and tended to view
the world that way. Chance, in his opinion, was an explanatory
last resort for those who didn't have the brains or the will to
think things through. But after what had happened yesterday
afternoon, he knew he just might have to revise that point of
view.

The chain of events — chances — began in his court late
yesterday morning in a break-and-enter case: two teenage boys
and a girl, all three well past the young offender stage. The
third prosecution witness had just raised his right hand, and
the "I swear" had come out with a bellow. Tom wasn't sure
whether the man was being defiant or just loud. Whichever it
was, with only those two words, he'd made everyone in the
court look up sharply.

The witness was a big man, maybe fifty, fifty-five, Tom
thought, with a huge distended beer belly. His belt was slung

so low it looked more like a truss than something to hold up his pants. The belly and the loud "I swear" triggered recall of a paragraph in the pretrial report. This must be Walter Hope, Tom realized, the one they called Whispering Hope — no wonder! He was the construction worker who claimed to have overheard the kids trying to deal goods on the patio of the Lagoon Saloon.

Tom tried to catch the eye of the young prosecuting attorney before she got started. Not only was she young, she was new, and this could turn into a lengthy examination. Sometime later, Tom was to acknowledge to himself that it was at this very point that "chance" might have taken over.

A double shot of chance, actually. The first unusual occurrence was that the Yankees played the Blue Jays that afternoon, one of those rare midweek 1:30 starts. The second was that Tom had tickets, and it really wasn't his turn for them. He and four others had a pair of seasons. They called themselves the Twenty Percent Club, for at the beginning of the schedule each year they divided the tickets five ways. Tom's Yankee game for this series would normally have been the next night, but weeks ago he'd made a trade. Chance?

Whatever the chain of circumstance, there was no way he was going to miss the first pitch no matter how slowly the wheels of justice might grind as a result, and so, very unobtrusively, he gave the high sign to Maurice Marchand standing at the back.

"Just a minute, Ms. Dankert." Tom caught the prosecutor before she stood up.

Maurice, the bailiff, saw the signal and walked urgently to the bench. Just as urgently, he whispered in Tom's ear, making very definitive movements with both hands. It was an old ploy that Tom Houghton rarely used, but, well, a Yankees game was a Yankees game.

"I'm afraid it will be necessary to adjourn," Tom announced to the court.

Maurice Marchand, meanwhile, had turned to face the courtroom and stood impassively with his arms folded.

"We will reconvene — how about an early start? Nine a.m. tomorrow?"

There were no objections.

Forty-five minutes later, His Honor was locking his car at a parking lot by the Skydome. Another dollop of chance? Well, maybe: it was the *last* space in the lot! Tom wasn't all that keen about leaving his car there. Just across the fence lay the remains of rubble from a demolished building. The workmen clearing it were on lunch. It meant dust and dirt, but to find another spot to park would also mean missing the first inning. Tom opted for dust and dirt.

Two hours later he saw the consequence of his decision, but another helping of chance made it a minor issue. It had been a dull game and Tom had left in the bottom of the eighth to beat the rush. After unlocking his car — actually, it wasn't *too* dirty — he straightened to take off his windbreaker, and there, not more than half a dozen paces away on the other side of the fence, was Whispering Hope! Any other time Tom would have paid little attention, but there was no ignoring or mistaking that huge gut.

Hope was standing by the wheel of a backhoe with two other men. The three were having one of those shouted conversations so typical of construction sites where the equipment noise makes communication difficult. Unlike Hope, his two companions — a lot younger, Tom noticed — wore ear protectors, but they were pushed up above their ears. Walter Hope's hands were cupped behind his. His hard hat was white, too, Tom noticed, while the others' were yellow.

Whatever the subject of the conversation — it appeared to be a joke, for all three guffawed when it ended — the two younger men turned away to pick up shovels. Tom watched Hope hitch his hands under his mighty belly and swing up into the seat of the backhoe. The cover flap of the exhaust pipe, which had been barely vibrating before, now clattered away like a flag gone mad as the big man drove up the revs and poised the bucket to scoop some rubble. This was a man who loved to wrestle his machine.

Tom opened his car door finally, and sat in. He was depressed. Not only a lousy game, he thought, but — was it chance? — I've run into a witness.

"Now what do I do?" He was talking to the steering wheel without seeing it. "Do I speak to Ms. Dankert in chambers tomorrow? Talk to the kids' counsel too? Well, before anything, I'm going back to read that pretrial report again. If I go right now, it'll take me till just after the evening rush."

He started the car and waited patiently for the engine to warm. From the driver's seat he could see the car was dirtier than he'd first thought.

What will Tom Houghton be looking for in the pretrial report? What is bothering him that he feels he may have to bring up with the two attorneys?

4

On Flight 701 from Hong Kong

IN ONE SENSE IT WAS just an afterthought, but it earned Ralph Ransom a commendation and enhanced his reputation considerably in the branch. Immediately after his brief acceptance speech at the annual awards dinner, Ralph was commended yet again — this time by the director personally — for the tactful and diplomatic way he had explained the reasoning that had led him to assign two teams to the airport for the arrival of the suspected smuggler. Others would have sent just one.

Essentially, it was his experience as head of the west coast section of Canada Customs Investigations Branch that had taught him — the hard way — that a flight from Hong Kong on a weekend invariably brought out large groups of welcomers, with a resulting level of bustle and activity that often confused surveillance teams. That's why he'd pressed the intercom on that wet Saturday morning last November after the call had come from the DEA in Seattle, and asked his secretary to call out the Cummings team.

11

And then he'd pressed it again immediately and said, "The Kavanagh team, too!"

Right away both teams wanted to know how the DEA (the American Drug Enforcement Agency) had gotten involved in a diamond-smuggling case. Ralph had to reply that he didn't know. He'd find out, but for the moment there was the more urgent business of acting on the tip and meeting Cathay Pacific's Flight 701, due in at Vancouver's International Airport from Hong Kong at 1320 hours PST.

For more than a year, the Investigations Branch, along with the RCMP, the Hong Kong police and Interpol had been gathering evidence on a diamond-smuggling ring whose operations started in Durban, passed through Singapore to Hong Kong, and then moved into North America via Vancouver. Ralph couldn't be absolutely sure that this tip was related to the ring. But he also couldn't take the chance of ignoring it.

All he had been able to get out of the rather surly informant in Seattle was "You and the Mounties got a live one on your diamond thing on the Cathay Pacific 701." There was no name and no photo. There couldn't even be an explanation of who or what or why. Ralph suspected — and he certainly had no intention of sharing this with the surveillance teams — that the reason for the surliness, not to mention the sparse information, could be traced back to the sloppiness of the DEA unit in Hong Kong. The Seattle man was sure ticked off. Ralph's reading of the situation was that the DEA had been running a sting in Hong Kong and it had turned sour. The tip, if it really turned out to be a tip, was probably an attempt to salvage something. In any case, all Ralph had on the "live one" was a physical description, and he knew he wouldn't even have gotten that if it hadn't been for the fact that the Seattle man owed him a few large favors.

He'd sent the Cummings and the Kavanagh teams out then, to identify and follow a "male, Chinese, maybe forty years old, about five foot seven, hair parted left, thick glasses — Coke bottles! — khaki suit two-piece, white shirt, no tie" who would be disembarking at 1320 hours from Cathay Pacific Flight 701.

On the way out, Iggie Kavanagh had stopped in the doorway to ask if they were supposed to watch for a drop or a pass or anything specific. Ralph didn't know whether to be sheepish and admit he didn't know, or pull rank and make Iggie wish he'd kept his big mouth shut.

He did neither and only said, "Just monitor in detail. Keep me current. I'll decide later what to do about him. *If anything,*" he added under his breath.

Shortly after that the first field call had come in, and it made Ralph sit up straight. *There were two subjects!* The point man of the Cummings team, dressed in the white coveralls of the clean-up crew, had picked up the subject immediately and handed him off at the gate to the number two. Then, as he headed for the lockers to strip off the coveralls and get to the luggage area, he almost gave everything away by staring in astonishment. Suzy Hammill, the point for Iggie Kavanagh's team was following *another* Chinese man who fitted the description perfectly! Suddenly the two-team decision by Ralph Ransom looked very good. But before Ralph could permit any self-satisfaction he still had to decide whether either subject was "a live one."

He was able to make that decision about an hour later when both Kavanagh and Cummings called in. Kavanagh was first.

"He went through young Turpin's counter," Iggie reported, referring to the newest uniformed customs officer they had at the airport. "The kid was good. Stamped him through. No fuss, but we got all the basics off the passport. What we've got is Won Lee of Kowloon... let's see... forty-five years old, purpose of visit business, speaks English. No North American stamps and he says this is his first visit here."

"Okay. Then?" Ralph was listening closely.

"He went straight to The Thomas Cook Foreign Exchange. Used his American Express for $300 Canadian. Then he bought a Vancouver city map at W. H. Smith. I think maybe he's a chocolate freak. Bought two Mars bars at the stand across from Thomas Cook's. Cabbed to the Bayshore... ah... used Checker seven-six-four. Then before he checked in he bought another Mars bar at the smoke shop in the lobby. And after he got his key he went back and got *two more*! Mars bars, I mean.

"He's in room 1014. An ordinary single... Oh, one thing. The guy's as hyper as can be. He sort of flits more than walks. In the Cook's lineup and again at the hotel his feet were tapping away all the time. He doesn't like waiting. Each time he bought the chocolate bars he just pumped out the change at the people on the register. It only takes him seconds to buy anything. Oh, yes. Almost forgot. Manager says he used American Express to check in. Staying two nights."

"I assume your team's in place if he leaves the room?" Ralph asked. "You need any help? Anybody compromised?"

"Yes, no and no." Iggie replied. "But he's been on the phone almost from the second he went into his room."

"Good work," Ralph said. "Stay on the line if you can. I've got Andy on four."

Andy Cummings' account was somewhat similar. The gate officer checking the passport, Jean Lajoie, identified one Huan Lee of Hong Kong, forty-one years old, in Canada for business reasons, very frequent traveler in the Orient — stamps on top of stamps in the passport. Never been to Canada or the U.S.

"Speaks good English, too," Andy said. "Least accordin' to the teller at th' Royal Bank. Cashed four hunnert bucks in traveler's checks... uh... uh... Thomas Cook, if that matters. Uh... they'll hold 'em till tumorruh 'f we want prints."

"I'll think that one over for a bit. We have time," Ralph said. He hesitated to press Andy for more. Andy Cummings' habit of overly casual speech was strictly a telephone phenomenon. He didn't talk that way in person and the inconsistency had always intrigued Ralph.

Andy didn't wait for a prompt, however. "Lessee... no more

14

stops at th' airport. Checker two-one-two to th' Hotel Van. Oh, yeah! Made a phone call from the lobby! Afore checkin' in. Strange, huh? Room's covered by traveler's check. He's in 414. Thassa suite. Booked fer two nights."

Andy paused, as though deciding whether to add more, and then did. "Funny thing. 'E's only got one small suitcase. Suzy checked with Cathay P. 'Tsall he checked on."

"You saw something wrong with that?" Ralph wanted to know.

"Naw... well... kinda skimpy for a guy 'n a *suite*!"

It was Ralph's turn to pause now. "Could be. Has he used the phone in his room yet?" he asked.

"Nope. We gonna tap?"

Ralph paused yet again.

"Andy?"

"Yeah?"

"Stay on the line, will you? I've got Iggie here, too."

"'Kay." Andy replied.

"I think," Ralph said, "we've got at least *one* live one!"

Ralph Ransom has a suspicion about one of the two men. Which one? And what has made him suspicious?

5

Trying to Find
Headquarters

WITH THE FOG SO THICK that visibility was limited to about
the length of a pair of outstretched arms, it was a real surprise
that Corporal Fogolin had found a road sign. Not that finding
it was going to do much good. The sign, like all the others in
the area, had been broken off and tossed away by the retreating
German forces. This one, however, had ended up in the ditch
instead of way off in a field somewhere, and Fogolin had
almost stumbled over it. His discovery gave the little group a
chance to rest for a moment while Captain Doyle moved up to
take a look at the thing for himself.

When Doug Doyle saw it, his heart missed a beat. It was —
or rather it had been — one of those overloaded signs the
French are so fond of using on rural roads. Short pieces of wood
with one end shaped like an arrow, nailed to the four sides of a
square post and pointing to every nearby city, hamlet, church
and place of geographical interest that could give the sponsoring community some importance. Lying there in the ditch, the
sign no longer appeared to have any value to anyone, least of

all a group of soldiers utterly lost in dense fog.

Some of the pieces were still attached. ST-AUBERT, where they were trying to go, was stuck straight into the ground as though to get there it would be necessary to dig straight down. On a broken piece under a clump of grass, Doug could see the letters CA. Must be Caen, he surmised. The sign to Vire lay on the ground, too, broken in half with the two parts still clinging together. The same was true for Flers. The one for Falaise — wherever that was — was unscathed. Bayeux was intact, too, as was Saint-Luc-Sud, but the one nailed perpendicular to it, Saint-Luc... something, was partly broken off. Someone had scribbled over the sign to Lisieux: "KÖLN 600 km". It had never occurred to Doug before that German soldiers might get homesick, too.

"What now, sir?" Corporal Fogolin broke in with precisely the question that Captain Doyle kept pushing away to the edges of his consciousness.

"Ah... ah... we take five minutes to rest" was Doug's hesitant reply. "You tell the others."

"Okay, sir."

"And no cigarettes! Even if we don't know where we are, there's no sense announcing ourselves to a sniper."

"Sir!" Corporal Fogolin backed up and in two steps was enveloped by the mist.

Doug sat down wearily. He held his wristwatch close to his face, moving his arm back and forth slowly. Although he'd had no night training, it hadn't taken him long to learn that in pitch blackness it was easier to read his timepiece that way.

Fifteen minutes past midnight. A new day, he realized — 19 July 1944. Only a week ago — *one week ago!* — he had been sitting at the Errant Piper on the outskirts of Leicester, trying to get a cute little American bird to understand that there was nothing at all quaint or unusual about English place names. She'd giggled almost uncontrollably when she'd learned he had been born in Stow-on-the-Wold but, to his irritation, didn't see anything the least bit unusual about the name of her own hometown, Cheektowaga, in the state of New York.

And he couldn't get her to see either that whether a car had a "boot" or a "trunk" it was all the same, or that having an "ice" wasn't any more or less civilized than having "ice cream."

Now he could show her! If only she were here now, so she could see how much better a word "cock-up" was for the mess they were in than any word the Americans had.

A right proper cock-up, too. In the first place he had no business leading men in a combat area. He was a captain, all right, and these American infantrymen had a real respect for him. Or at least wariness; they certainly weren't as casual as they had been with their own major.

But I'm a cryptographer! What do I know about combat? Doug Doyle kept having to push down the fear that thought produced.

The only reason he was even here was to link up with Montgomery's headquarters staff. They wanted decoding expertise.

This whole affair, however, had been a cock-up from the beginning. He'd left Leicester on six hours' notice for Portsmouth in order to be ferried over to Juno Beach. There the Canadians were to move him up to Monty's headquarters. But his ship diverted first to Southampton and then landed at Sword Beach! No one there, of course, knew or cared who he was, and that took even more time to straighten out.

Yesterday — no, the day before yesterday now — he'd finally been shifted to Utah Beach to join an American infantry major who was being posted to Montgomery's headquarters as liaison. That's when the cock-up changed from ordinary to extraordinary. He and the major and three others overloaded a jeep and set out at dawn yesterday from what Doug now realized was the relative security of Utah Beach. The plan was to make Monty's headquarters by noon. At Bayeux they were held up by MPs but had a ringside seat for an aerial bombardment that made Doug's few nights in London during the Blitz seem pretty mild.

When they were free to leave, by late afternoon, they could hear but not see the battle in the far distance. Ironically, several thousand miles away, people listening to their radios knew more than they did: that along the River Orne that morning, General Montgomery had launched a major tank offensive. It was intended to move the Germans off the heights to clear the way to Paris, and Monty planned to accomplish that by evening. Unfortunately the Germans had other ideas, and the biggest tank force the western Allies had put together thus far in the war was stopped dead in its tracks. Vaguely aware that something big was going on, yet uneasily shut out of all this history in the making, was Captain Douglas Doyle, cryptographer.

At dusk the fog had rolled in, and with it came tragedy. After about two hours of crawling along the road with the jeep in first gear, the major had called a halt to cool the engine and give everyone a chance for roadside relief. He was the last one out and stepped on a land mine. He died instantly. By diving instinctively for the ditches the others saved themselves, because the jeep went up two seconds later.

The cock-up was then total. They had no idea where they were, the maps had burned, the radio was gone, the fog was if anything getting thicker, and Doug Doyle whispered to himself in disbelief, "Good God! I'm in command!"

That was about 10 P.M. Since then, they had walked along the ditch, Doug's first order. The Jerries might have mined the road, he reasoned, but the ditches... well, odds are they didn't have the time or the inclination. Now, with Corporal Fogolin finding the road sign, the cock-up had reached a turning point.

Doug scrambled up to the road on his hands and knees. "Up here, chaps!" he called softly. "We can walk the road now, I think."

Immediately they gathered around.

Doug continued, "Single file again. I'll lead. We turn down this road."

Corporal Fogolin stepped closer to peer through the fog at Doug's face. "Turn, sir? Here, sir?"

He got a reassuring nod from Doug. "Yes, here." He paused. "Don't worry, Corporal. What's the expression? 'No sweat'?" To himself he added, "Peculiar way to talk."

Captain Doug Doyle has apparently been able to determine where the group should go. How has he done this?

6

The Case of the Disappearing Credit Card

OTHER THAN THEIR MOTHER, JULIE Iseler was probably the only person who knew how to tell the Saint twins apart. Their father apparently couldn't, and certainly no one else could — except maybe Tammy Hayward, for like Julie she'd cut their hair from time to time. The clue was that Peter Saint had a double crown, a double "cowlick" it was sometimes called, but his brother, Paul, had only a single one.

Both boys' crowns made their hair exceptionally difficult to style. Cut too short, the hair at the top of their heads stuck out every which way. If it was left long, the cowlicks tended to dictate what happened to the rest of the head. That, in any case, was academic. The Saints, Peter and Paul, had short hair. It was one of the few battles — perhaps the only one — their mother regularly won.

However, the problems associated with periodically realigning the Saint boys' mops were not the only considerations that weighed on Julie's mind this morning as she looked over the day's appointments. (The twins were down for just before noon.)

21

Yes, their hair was hard to cut, but, well, Tammy could do one and she the other. What made the day ahead seem so long — she looked up at the clock; it was only 8:50 A.M. — was that a visit from the Saints was just not the kind of thing to brighten one's day.

"Hell on Reeboks," one of Julie's regulars had dubbed them, and that may well have been a mild view, for these two did everything possible to give the lie to their surname. They were only nine years old, duplicates of each other even down to their ample sprays of freckles, and they had already established a reputation for themselves that guaranteed a shudder at the news of their imminent arrival.

They were well known at Hair Apparent, and regarded with wariness. Not without cause, either. One of them had pinched Julie last spring as she'd bent to retrieve a pair of scissors. That's how she'd found out that, unlike his brother, Paul was left-handed. During the same visit Peter had almost baked Mrs. Horschak by surreptitiously turning the big bell dryer to MAX and resetting the timer. "Double trouble" was far too mild a metaphor for Peter and Paul Saint. No one used it anymore.

The front door to Hair Apparent opened and the movement of air shook the hanging wall dividers. It was Tammy.

"Sorry." Tammy had an embarrassed smile. "My car."

Working for Julie was Tammy's first full-time job. She was also the proud owner of a first car, which unless its record changed was soon to become a former car.

"No problem, Tammy." Julie returned the smile. The two of them got along especially well, and just seeing her walk in was bringing back Julie's innate good cheer. She held the smile and watched Tammy hang up her nylon shell jacket, then bump her arm on the nearest wall divider.

The smile turned into a laugh. "You can't get used to those things, either," Julie said. "Don't feel bad. I've already walked into the one by the cash this morning. You'll be happy to know the people from TBS are coming this afternoon to turn them around the right way."

TBS stood for Tasteful but Secure, a decorating service that Julie had hired for the first major renovation of her salon. Neither she nor Tammy was particularly pleased with the result. Before the change, Julie could work at her chair — the center one of three — and, in any of the big mirrors these chairs faced, monitor the entrance door, the waiting area, the cash register, even the two sinks and spare chair, which in that sequence took up the wall to her left.

The new hanging dividers changed all that. Suspended by chains from the ceiling, these huge pieces of Lucite formed a more-or-less wall between the working area and the waiting area. The idea, Julie granted, made some sense. The panels created two rooms, in a way, out of one big one. They permitted flow-through — in theory at least — for by turning sideways you could slip between panels and "walk through the wall." And the real bonus, supposedly, was that the panels were specially treated to permit a kind of translucent see-through from one side, while the other side reflected. The purpose was to give Julie and Tammy's patrons a sense of privacy in the chairs, while permitting the two stylists to see through to the entrance and waiting areas.

Fine. Except that the workers had hung the panels the wrong way. Customers in the waiting room could see into the work area, but the only way Julie could see them from her center chair, short of backing up a few steps and sticking her head through the wall, was via her mirror and then the mirror in front of the spare chair on the side wall. Not terribly secure. And neither Julie nor Tammy was sure it was all that tasteful, either.

"You've got Mrs. Goodman in a few minutes, Tammy." It was time for business. "Perm. And there's a whole lineup of kids. Not surprising. It's back-to-school time."

"Oh, yeah!" Tammy's eyes widened. "It's going to be so strange watching everyone else go, without going, too!"

Julie hadn't heard her. She was absorbed in the appointment book. "George from the bank... Either one of us can do him.

Wash and cut. He'll be in a hurry as usual. Mrs. Morelli, the Saint twins, then…"

Tammy lit up at that. "Did you *hear* what those kids did on that Vacation Bible School bus? They took the bolts out of the driver's seat. While she was driving! I don't know how they managed it. Anyway, the first time she braked she went right under the steering wheel! It's a wonder —"

The wall dividers swung in sympathy to the opening door. Mrs. Goodman had arrived for her perm. Julie and Tammy both went to greet her. Thoughts of the Saint twins faded, for Mrs. Goodman was their favorite senior. To both of them, she was "just a doll."

"Oh, my! You've changed things," the old lady said in her sweet, ingenuous way. She really *was* a doll. "Well, it doesn't matter, dear." She had turned her attention to Tammy. "You're still here, and that's all that matters. Shall we get started?"

Tammy led Mrs. Goodman to her chair, to the right of Julie's. The door opened again. The dividers shook. It was a mother with three very small children. For a moment, Julie was perplexed. Only one of them was school age. Oh, yes, the Beaumonts. First one off to kindergarten. This was going to be an important haircut.

That was the last opportunity for contemplation, because things then got very busy. By the time George from the bank came "to be squeezed in," both Julie and Tammy were a full appointment behind.

And the Saints were on time.

Julie slipped quickly through the wall to explain that things were running just a bit behind. Maybe fifteen minutes.

"Oh… oh… now… oh…" Mrs. Saint lived perpetually on the edge of crisis, and Julie's news threatened to push her over.

"Oh… goodness. Now… oh… okay… okay… This is what we'll do."

Mrs. Saint spoke only in the first person plural — or the

royal *we* — Julie could never figure out which. She also had a habit of swaying from the waist in a kind of oval bobbing pattern not unlike the mating ritual of some large water bird. The bobbing began to float her toward the door.

"We have one more errand, so we can do that. Now, boys, we won't leave those chairs, right?" To Julie she added, "Fifteen minutes? We'll be right back."

Julie backed up a few steps. The boys were paying no attention whatsoever to their mother's admonitions. One of them was busily but carefully engaged with a red felt-tipped marker, outlining a "tattoo" of a dragon that had been dyed onto the crook of his elbow. Every few seconds he'd check the one on his brother's arm to be sure his duplication was precise. The Saints had apparently visited Unter's Variety Store on the way, for the tattoo was the stick-on type that comes in packs of gum. Despite her mild concern over what else the twins might do with the red marker, Julie couldn't help noting the similarity in the two boys' artwork.

She turned back to resume the final trim on George, and promptly walked into one of the panels. The resulting *thunk* startled everyone except Peter and Paul Saint. They had gotten up and moved to different chairs the instant their mother left. With an empty chair between them to serve as working surface they began to unwrap what looked like enough chocolate bars to zit an entire junior high class for life...

None of this bothered Julie for the moment. She had George to finish and things were getting even further behind. With all the activity she was just a few breaths shy of being frazzled *and now the telephone rang!*

One thing TBS had put in that was going to stay for sure was the roam phone receiver on the back of Julie's chair. This innovation meant she could answer calls without leaving her customer; because of the big mirror, she didn't even have to lose eye contact.

She gave George an I-know-this-is-taking-longer-than-it-should look, as she picked up the receiver and balanced it on her shoulder to talk. Now she had both hands free to continue with him.

"Is this Julie or Tammy?" It was the easily recognizable, inviting voice of Mrs. Goodman. "I can never tell you young girls apart on the telephone."

"It's Julie, Mrs. Goodman. How can I help you?"

"Oh, thank you, dear. I think I left my credit card at your place. It wasn't in my purse when I got home. I think when I..."

Automatically Julie looked up to take in the cash register first. Right there! A VISA card right on the cash drawer ledge below the keys. Funny they hadn't seen it before.

"Yes, it's here, Mrs. Goodman. I'm sure it's yours. Just hang on a sec and I'll — Mrs. Goodman! I'll call you right back!"

"Tammy!" Julie set the roam phone on the shelf below the mirror and picked up the blow dryer. She didn't want George to hear, so she turned it on near his ear.

"Those Saint kids!" she said to Tammy. "Paul. The single crown? He just took Mrs. Goodman's VISA off the cash. I saw him in the mirror. We're going to go over quietly and get it from them before their mother comes back, or she'll have a stroke! We'll both go. You just stand in front of Peter. I'll get the card from Paul."

Tammy's voice was urgent. "How do you know it's Paul? Did he turn his head?"

"No!" Julie replied. "It was the tattoo!"

They slipped through the wall, Tammy leading.

"But they *both* have a tattoo!" Her whisper was very loud.

Julie was calm but determined. "It's Paul," she said.

How can Julie be so confident in her identification?

7

A Badly Planned Saturday?

THE SCENE, WERE IT NOT for the sad story associated with it, would have been idyllic. One of those nature segments that appears at least once a night on public television. Or a piece from a commercial by a conservation group.

It's the birds, Jeff Baldwin concluded, that make one sensitive to just how peaceful it is up here. The only sound, except for the occasional click/whirr of his camera, came from the birds. There was also, now that he paid attention to it, the steady rush of the wind, but it, too, was peaceful as it sieved through the pines. More a background than anything else. A background for the birds.

From where he sat on the carpet of pine needles, Jeff could see six — no, seven; no, *eight!* — different species: jays; chickadees, of course; finches; a pair of woodpeckers. He could hear a cardinal even if he couldn't see it. Nuthatches: two varieties of them —

Suddenly his cataloging was interrupted by the mildest and most silent and simple change. It put a chill on things. A cloud had slid over the sun, and what had been so warm and inviting only seconds before — a perfect example of nature's grace — seemed to become gloomy and ominous. Even the birds quietened, in sympathy with the mood. Or did their silence create the mood?

Whatever. It reminded Jeff of why he was here. He picked up his camera to check the settings. There was sand on the edge of the lens cover and some pine needles stuck in the buckle of the carrying strap. As he lifted the camera to his eye, a tiny insect added to his unease by settling on his ear. He brushed at it. No effect. Again. It wouldn't go away. Then he realized it was only a thin curl of bark from the top of the stump that formed his backrest.

In the brief moment when all that was happening, the sun came back, just as suddenly as it had disappeared. The cardinal began to sing again and the wind softened. But Jeff's good feeling was gone now. His sense of peace had been exchanged for one of unrest and the press of duty. He was here to do a job.

Jeff Baldwin was a reporter, and he was way up here at this elevation to do a follow-up on the Turner-Burnside rescue. Two hours ago he had left a rented 4 x 4 at the end of an abandoned logging road and scrambled on foot up a very rough hiker's path to this — well, call it a clearing, he thought. Actually, it wasn't a natural clearing; it was really a growth of young pine, regenerating after a fire that had cleared out the area more than thirty years ago.

What made it a clearing was that about twenty or twenty-five of the young trees had been cut. All of them like the one Jeff was sitting against. Neatly, with a crosscut saw.

The trees had been used to make the Turners and the Burnsides a crude shelter. Jeff couldn't see it from where he was sitting now, but he knew it was only a few steps away, around the knoll to the left. He had photographed it only a couple of minutes ago, taking particular care to get the light setting right. He wanted all the dead pine needles on the trees to show. This would be the big spread picture. It would help the story.

The Turners and the Burnsides were snowmobilers. Last January they had set out on their machines for a Saturday of "trailing." It was an excursion marked by disaster: disaster of their own making, reinforced by bad luck.

To begin with, they had not told anyone — least of all the forest service — where they were going, or even that they were going at all! They weren't reported missing therefore until the following Monday afternoon, and the search hadn't begun until Wednesday because of the bad weather. No one even knew where to look until a helicopter crew spotted the Burnsides' jeep at the foot of Ebbett's Pass. The Pass had been closed since November.

Even so, things might have turned out all right for the two couples, but a combination of circumstance piled up on them like the snow that had begun to fall that Saturday afternoon. First the drive belt broke on Jeannie Burnside's Citation. That should not have been a particular problem, since all snowmobilers carry an extra drive belt. It's automatic. Like a spare tire. Except Jeannie didn't have one, and hers was the only Citation. The others each drove a V-Max.

Then the storm hit. Naturally, since the two couples hadn't told the forest service they were going up (or asked permission: the proper procedure) it follows that they hadn't bothered to check with the weather service, either. By the time they got here, to what was now a clearing, a storm had dumped mounds of fresh snow on top of what was already a record winter's snowfall. Dan Turner later described the fresh snow as over his head in spots: too much even for snowmobiles. That's when they built the shelter. Mark Burnside had a mountain pack — hence the saw — and they holed up to wait out the storm.

At first there was no reason to worry. Jeannie Burnside might not have carried an extra drive belt, but she was notorious for packing way too much food on all these trips, and this time was no exception. For a short period, according to Dan, it was almost fun. Neither couple had children or any immediate have-to-get-home responsibility. There was food and shelter. Three snowmobiles worked, and they weren't lost.

But Marie Turner got sick. Food poisoning, the autopsy said later. By Sunday night she was dehydrated and delirious. Her pulse was thready and she was drifting in and out of consciousness. So on Monday morning as soon as there was light, Mark Burnside set out on foot down the mountain, using snowshoes he had fashioned from pine branches and vinyl strips cut from the snowmobile seats.

His body was found when the snow melted, about two months ago, at the bottom of a long straight drop. His neck was broken and so was his left arm. Dan Turner speculated that with the poor visibility in the storm, Mark must have walked right out into air. It was too bad he hadn't waited. Only a few hours after the Burnsides' jeep was spotted, a helicopter was hovering over the clearing and winching out Dan Turner and Jeannie Burnside. A quick second trip was necessary to recover Marie Turner's body. By that time she had been dead almost thirty-six hours.

Jeff Baldwin had been the only reporter to get near the scene. He'd talked his way onto the 'copter that came back for Marie's body, and his story and pictures had been picked up by every wire service in North America and two or three in Europe. In fact it occurred to Jeff that by coming up here to get a feel for his follow-up story (there was going to be a big magazine spread this time) he was also one of the first people, if not the very first, to visit the spot since the week of the rescue.

He patted his vest to be sure he still had the extra film. He'd need it. But what concerned him most right now was whether he should go to the police first when he got back down. If he told his editor first what he had learned up here, she would insist on running the story, and nuts to the police.

But publishing the story first could easily condemn Dan Turner or Jeannie Burnside or both. And what he had, Jeff knew, wasn't *absolute* proof. Fishy, though. Very fishy. He wondered what Dan and Jeannie meant to each other, what kind of relationship they had. The answer to that might help with his decision.

What has Jeff Baldwin learned at this mountain scene that is making him debate whether to go first to the police with the information, or to his editor?

8

From *Sine Timore*
(The official newsletter of the National Association of Security Services)

WINNER OF THIS MONTH'S TROJAN Horse Award is Stephen James, vice president and general manager of Vigil Security in Niagara. Stephen proved the aptness of his company name by breaking an industrial theft ring at a principal client: Category Tool & Die Makers in Monmouth.

Category, as readers of *Sine Timore* will be well aware, has been plagued by a rash of product theft, particularly of precision cold-rolled steel parts. The situation in this company has been aggravated, too, by what are possibly the worst employee-management relations in the Dakota Industrial Basin. A record three wildcat strikes last year followed what was supposed to be the resolution of a six-month legal walkout. The spark in the case of each walkout was shop steward Horace Cater's contention that Category management was union-baiting in its attempts to stop the thefts.

Before Stephen and Vigil Security were brought in, as agreed to by both union and management, Category Tool & Die had been using the random search method, which, in seven attempts, had turned up only one uncertain suspect.

Stephen's first step when his company accepted the contract was to halt the random searches, then establish an inventory control marking system. Hand counts of inventory, compared with computer printouts, confirmed the company's belief that the theft was taking place principally at the close of shifts. Certain workers on the floor were apparently walking out with the heavy parts concealed on their persons or in carryons.

Since the company had already tried a security X-ray scanning system (which triggered two of the wildcat walkouts) it was obvious to Stephen that this method was not ideal. The third walkout had occurred when management initiated a hand search system of the duffle bags that all shop floor employees carry from their work stations to the change-and-shower room or directly out to the parking lot, as they choose.

Every single employee responded in the next shift by carrying his or her personal items — and, management alleged, stolen parts — in cardboard boxes sealed with tape. Cater acknowledged that this was his idea, and that the union had supplied the cartons. As Stephen James explained to *Sine Timore*, breaking the taped seal on these bread-box-sized cartons constituted violation of privacy in the eyes of the union — a grievable action — and justified the "collective response" (which is what Cater prefers to call the walkouts). These were the conditions when Vigil Security took over at Category, but Stephen James was able to crack the situation to the satisfaction of both management and union.

His solution involved some minor reconstruction in the exit area where employees punched out their time cards. Before Vigil's involvement, Category workers at the end of a shift would walk through a pair of electronically responsive doors into a lobby, then through another pair of doors to the change-and-shower room. Before passing through the first pair of doors, workers would pull their personal time cards from a wall rack, insert them into the time clock to be stamped, then return them to a rack on the other side of the clock.

Stephen's strategy was to move the time clock and the second rack to the lobby. On only the third day of this system, Stephen was sufficiently certain of the culprits to detain them and open their sealed boxes in the presence of steward Horace Cater.

The success was total. Two of the guilty workers independently identified key members of the theft ring to Stephen in the presence of both management and union. The guilty parties are facing prosecution, and Category Tool & Die no longer has a theft problem.

Sine Timore congratulates Stephen James and Vigil Security, winners of the T.H.A. (No photos are published at request of Mr. James.)

How was Stephen James able to pick out the workers who were stealing parts?

9

"Could Be the Biggest Thing Since Tutankhamen"

"WHERE?"

Thomas Arthur Jones had not intended to shout into the telephone, but the conversation that up to now had occupied only half his attention suddenly engaged him completely.

He had been deeply engrossed in a final proofreading of his paper on the Olduvai Gorge skeletons. (Jones felt the Leakeys had seriously misinterpreted the significance of these remains; this was to be his third published contribution to the debate, which he himself had begun with his presentation six years ago at the annual meeting of the Learned Society.)

"Where?" He repeated. "Say that again!"

The amount of interest in his voice was a full turnabout from the desultory "Jones" with which he'd first answered. That was his standard opening: polite but uninviting, a response he'd perfected over his past two years as Professor of the Schliemann Chair of Archaeology at the Smithsonian. By sounding preoccupied, he could filter out and quickly dismiss the calls he didn't want. That was just about all of them.

This particular one had begun terminally, for to "Jones" the caller at the other end had said, confidently, "Tom Jones? T. A. Jones?"

There was a chilly pause before Jones replied, "This is *Dr. Jones, yes.* Thomas Arthur Jones."

The voice changed immediately from confident to supplicant. "Dr. Jones. Of course. Dr. Thomas Jones, ah... ah... 'Impact of Andean Orogeny on Fossil Distribution in the Oligocene Era.' *That* Dr. Jones, right?"

This citing of one of his early papers had kept the eminent Dr. Jones on the line, yet the substance of the call immediately reversed things again, for Jones was convinced he was being sucked into a joke. Thomas Arthur Jones had little time for jokes.

The voice identified itself as Jimmy Strachan, associate editor of one of the country's largest newsmagazines, and then proceeded to announce that a hiker — a rock climber, actually — had come to him with a tale of discovering a Stone Age tribe, or what appeared to be a Stone Age tribe. For Jones, that was the tip-off: he knew this was definitely a joke. Until Strachan told him where the discovery had been made. That's when Prof. Jones shouted into the receiver.

He did it once more.

"*Where?*"

"Staten Island." Strachan risked a rude response by repeating phonetically, "Stat-en I-land."

"I am not a simpleton, Mr. Strachan. Nor am I hearing-impaired." Jones spoke very deliberately. "We *are* talking about Isla de Los Estados, are we not? You wouldn't have the temerity to pretend that in New York harbor..."

"Dr. Jones, *please.*" This time it was Jimmy Strachan's turn for a little one-upmanship. That he'd scored a point or two was evident in Jones's grudging but apologetic reply.

"All right. But you understand that as a government-sponsored institution we have just about anyone calling here and I simply don't… well… I'm sure you understand."

"We get them, too, Dr. Jones." Strachan's tone had moved to the now-we-share-a-bond level. "And that's exactly how I first treated this man's proposal. I felt — you know — Stone Age tribe, indeed! But you should see his photographs! That's what kept me from tossing him out. You see, I don't know much about the Stone Age. Fact is, the only real reference point I've got is that movie — you know, ah — *Quest for Fire?*"

Thomas Arthur Jones just grunted.

"Anyway, his pictures will sell you, I'm sure." Strachan was speaking more confidently and confidentially. He knew he had Jones's interest now. "This guy, he's into archaeology in an amateur kind of way, but what he wants is money. Sorry. I'm getting ahead of myself. The guy — never mind his name for right now — he's a Brit. He's been going to the Falkland Islands ever since the war there. Something to do with compensation for the sheep farmers because of the war. Anyway, he's a rock climber, and while he was there on one of his trips he popped over to Tierra del Fuego."

"Quite a pop." Jones interrupted. "That's got to be over five hundred miles."

"Yes… ah —" Strachan was thrown a bit off stride — "ah… I understand Fuego's supposed to be a real score if you're a climber. Anyway, to make a long story short, he got himself over to Staten Island… ah… Isla de las Es-es."

"*Los* Estados," Jones filled in. "It's almost spot on the intersection of the fortieth parallel and sixty-five degrees."

There was a pause. Advantage Jones.

"Okay. Right. Anyway, the island's where he discovered the Stone Age tribe — ah… the *alleged* tribe." His voice wound up again. "But you've gotta see the pictures! Anyway, what he wants is $100,000 for an exclusive."

Thomas Arthur Jones reflected for a second or two on the $1,500 that had accompanied the Arthur Evans Prize he was awarded last year.

"... and what we would like you to do, Tom — *Dr. Jones!* — is verify the discovery for us before we spend those kind of bucks." There was a tiny break before he picked up again, his voice just ever so much less assertive. "We... ah... we'd need to know your fee first, Dr. Jones. Of course expenses are covered."

Thomas Jones looked at his paper on the Leakeys. He'd only been to South America once. A month at Iguassu Falls had come to nothing that time because the Paraguayans and the Argentines had had a falling out over the project. This island was a good two-thousand-plus miles south of that. It would be three or four days' travel — one way. A week at the site. And the publications! The question was... what kind of fee would a news-magazine pay?

Strachan ventured tentatively, "We're asking you, Dr. Jones, because... well... you're the real expert on anything post-Pleistocene, aren't you?"

Whether it was his intent or not, associate editor Strachan had played a very high trump. He'd said the one thing that Thomas Arthur Jones, B.Sc., M.A.(Oxon.), Ph.D., F.R.S.C., could not set aside. And he'd cut the fee in half.

"I must say, Mr. Strachan, it certainly does sound intriguing. I guess I could do it. Now, my fee is really incidental. I'll accept a per diem of, say, $300? But you must understand, I only fly first class." That was a quick addition. Jones congratulated himself. "I imagine I'll have to go through Rio and Buenos Aires."

The delight in his caller's voice told Jones he could have nailed down a much higher per diem.

"Excellent, Dr. Jones. I'll have one of our people in Washington come to you today if that's all right, and I'll courier the photographs. They'll be there tomorrow morning."

The conversation ended a few minutes later with various pleasantries and expressions of mutual respect. Just in time, too; Jones had a meeting down the hall. He walked as quickly as he could — Thomas Arthur Jones did not run — thinking how timely that call had been. The meeting was a regular department affair to discuss what success the faculty was having in the never-ending search for grants and awards. This Staten Island thing could become big.

The following morning, however, Jones's absorption in the Olduvai Gorge paper shifted the Stone Age tribe to the back of his mind — until the photographs arrived. He was bent over his drafting table when the department secretary came in with a package that soon took up the whole of the working surface.

"Gorgeous. Excellent!" Jones muttered when he pulled the pictures out of the slit in the side of the package. Most of them were blowups, in black-and-white.

The first several shots were of the inhabitants. They certainly appeared Stone Age: short stature, very wrinkled skin on the older ones — backs and stomachs, especially. That was good. So were the stooped shoulders. There were missing teeth. One of the younger ones had a broken arm that hadn't healed correctly. The skin was very black, almost Australian aboriginal, Jones thought. He didn't know quite what to make of that. Many of them had that furtive, uncertain, trapped-small-animal look he'd seen so often in the faces of primitive people who encounter something — especially technology — that is beyond their comprehension or frame of reference.

Shots of the living area had been taken with several different lenses. A fisheye had been used to produce an all-encompassing view of a very large-mouthed but shallow cave on the — Jones turned the photograph forty-five degrees — it would have to be the north side of a solitary mountain. Hill, really. A fire-pit took up most of the floor area at the arch of the cave mouth. Leading away from the entrance, the ground was level and well swept. In two subsequent shots, a larger view of this area showed children playing a game that appeared not unlike soccer. He couldn't see a ball, though.

Interior shots suggested the group had been here a long time, and planned to stay. Food hung from slings tied to stalactites, well out of reach of the dogs and children Jones saw in the pictures. There was a lot of it: drying meat, what looked like onions, a kind of rutabaga, some other vegetation — spices? medications? — but more meat than anything else. They were certainly successful hunters. That would also account for the skins they wore.

The floor was remarkably clean. Space seemed to have been divided into living areas with tiny walls of smooth stones. The walls were symbolic, for none of them were more than ankle height. One of the most interesting features was a pool, apparently fed from an underground stream. It drained away through a crack at the rear of the cave. Clearly, the pool was an important reason for the choice of the cave.

The rock climber had used a strong flash for these shots, for there was no rear entrance/exit to provide light back there. On several shots the flash had reflected off shiny objects arranged in geometric patterns. Bones, perhaps? Flint would reflect. Maybe something of religious significance to them.

The final set was presumably of the entire population. They looked ludicrously similar to school class photos, the kind of shot of the third grade in which one of the girls in the front row inevitably forgets to put her knees together. Or a boy in the back row discovers for the first time in three years that the building has a roof and he turns to give it a full scientific examination just as the photographer presses the button. These shots were taken outside the cave, to the left of the entrance. Behind the inhabitants, the surface was again level and clear, just like the area out front, as far as the camera could see.

An aerial shot confirmed that this was true all the way around the cave. The tribe had evidently opted for security over protection from the elements; they wanted to be able to see a good distance in every direction. Still, Jones acknowledged, the whole terrain was like that as far as he knew. Too cold by far for dense vegetation in any case.

Thomas Arthur Jones sighed. It would have been an interesting trip. He looked through the entire lot of pictures again and then went to his desk to find Jimmy Strachan's telephone number. Fascinating, in fact. But Jones's sense of ethics wouldn't let him go any further without telling his potential client that this was very unlikely to be a Stone Age tribe, that indeed it was far more likely to be a flat-out fraud.

"Oh, well —" he picked up the receiver "— at least I get to give the Leakey paper in Edinburgh. Maybe I can find a couple of interesting malts."

Why is Dr. Jones quite certain that the rock climber has not discovered a Stone Age tribe?

10

A Report on Conditions
at Scutari

IN FORTY-TWO YEARS OF bearing witness to the follies of humankind, Bill Lacroix had never felt so totally, utterly, helpless and frustrated. The immediate cause — of several — was that the soldier in front of him was dying, and he could do nothing at all about it. Septicemia from an untreated bayonet wound had taken over the young fusilier's entire body and was about to win the lad's final battle. No more than eighteen, Bill thought, if that. He doesn't deserve to die here. Not in this filth.

Bill bent over the soldier and put his hand on the boy's forehead. It was burning hot with the fever that tore away at the body. The irony of it all — the terrible, dreadful irony — was that the wound hadn't even come from the enemy. No Russian had caused this.

The soldier was a private in the 90th Light Infantry. He still wore the uniform; there had been no attempt to take it off or to change it as his condition had worsened over the past few days. In the boredom of the trenches outside Sebastopol, he and several others had been fooling with their bayonets. It wasn't much of a cut, but here in Scutari, in this warehouse that passed for a hospital, or across the Black Sea in Crimea, a scratch could be as fatal as a musket ball in the gut. Already, death from disease was taking away British soldiers four times as fast as the fight-ing. That was the deeper cause of Bill Lacroix's anger.

"This un's gone, guv'."

Bill turned to look at the orderly standing in the aisle. The man was almost completely covered from shoulders to knees by a huge apron. It seemed to be more appropriate for a tannery than a hospital. But then, it was easier to wipe blood and bits of flesh from leather than from cotton, and this orderly had come from the surgery in the next building. He was serving a two-week punishment for drunkenness. A burly fellow, Bill noted. Good thing, probably. His job was to kneel on the wounded and hold them down as the surgeons extracted bullets and shrapnel, or amputated, or as often as not, simply hacked.

The orderly stood there, tapping the forehead of the soldier in the cot behind Bill. "'E's gone," the man repeated, pushing the dead one's eyelids closed with two blood-encrusted fingers.

Several hours before, an officer had reluctantly instructed the orderly to escort Bill around the hospital. Although he was non-military, Bill represented the *Times* Fund, and potentially he had clout. The high command here in Turkey was beginning to appreciate the power of public opinion.

Bill forced himself to look at the dead soldier in the bed behind him. This man too still wore his tunic, unbuttoned and lying open, and Bill could see the mulberry rash that covered the skin. Typhus. He shuddered. There was no end to the awfulness here.

A rumble of thunder drew his attention back to the soldier with the bayonet wound. There were no walls in shed no. 14, and the young lad's head lay right under the edge of the roof-line.

Bill walked to the foot of the bed. "Help me pull this into the aisle a bit," he said to the orderly. "At least he can die without rain in his face."

"Right, guv'." The orderly helped Bill pull the bed into the aisle a few inches.

"Let's do all of them like his," Bill said. "If that storm is anything like the one yesterday…" He didn't bother to finish.

The two of them worked together, pulling alternate beds into the aisle, eight on one side, the same on the other. The orderly was quite willing. This was better duty than the agony and screaming in the surgery.

"You th' Russell chap, guv'?" he wanted to know. William Howard Russell had been the *Times'* special correspondent whose reports from the field had ignited public opinion in London, and had even attracted the attention of Queen Victoria. His accounts of the dreadful conditions and over-crowding at the huge Barracks Hospital in Scutari had triggered two immediate results: the arrival in Turkey of a group of women under the charge of a nurse the military command referred to as "that dreadful Nightingale woman"; and the establishment of the *Times* Fund for the benefit of wounded soldiers.

"No. My name's Lacroix." Bill bent over to pick a soiled dressing off the floor of the aisle, then straightened immediately. He hadn't realized how foul the smell was at bed level. At that height, the smell of gangrene and suppurating wounds was overlain by the stench of men lying in their own soil.

"Be ye with t'other chap, then?" The orderly had that curious insouciance of the street.

"What other chap?" Bill was instantly on guard. He had thought he was the only civilian inspecting here.

"The one this mornin'. The toff. 'Ad t'show 'im round, too. Right proper one, 'im. All fancy like." The orderly knuckled his dirty finger against a nostril and blew with great vigor. "Didn't bother 'im none in 'ere, it didn't." He paused to clear the other side in the same way. "Sat there b'th'door. Wrote nigh an hour 'e did. 'Im 'n' 'is fancy ink pots 'n' all." He repeated the expurgation at the first nostril. "'Spect 'e's comin' back. Left it all 'ere when old Rags 'imself come by. Mus' be friends, 'im 'n' the toff."

"Rags" was Lord Raglan, the one-armed commander-in-chief of the British army in the Crimea. Bill's antennae were pulsing now. What was Raglan doing here? He never went near the wounded if he could help it.

"'E sat 'ere," the orderly said, "over 'ere," he added, wiping his hands on the tannery apron with more than the usual effort as he walked toward a portable mahogany writing table at the entranceway. Bill wondered why he hadn't noticed it before; its pristine elegance stood out so in this crowded ward of dirt and death.

With great care the orderly nudged a sheet of cream linen writing paper. "'Spect ye c'n read, guv'."

It wasn't meant sarcastically. The orderly was just as curious as Bill to know what was written there.

Bill leaned over the table, then bent very close. In spite of the fact that Shed 14 had no walls, the light was very dim. Before him lay the first page of a letter — no, a report! It was written in a careful, deliberate script.

29 January 1855
The Barracks Hospital, Scutari

Sidney Herbert, Esq.,
My dear Sidney,

I sit, as I write, in Ward Number Fourteen, where our brave soldiers recover from their wounds. Regrettably, not all will do so for such are the fortunes of war. Nevertheless, all is done that can be done. Indeed, there are those here, whose station in life has been such that the accoutrements available to them, at the point of their extremity, represent an experience of considerable novelty.

From my vantage, I can observe the care of our stout fellows. They recline in two rows in this ward, embracing a passageway from which the ministrations of the attendants are delivered. It is quite orderly. In each row, eight heads point outward; eight pairs of feet point in. Very like the parade square at Lockham, which I am sure you remember, as I do, with fondness.

Barracks Hospital here in Scutari, contrary to ill-founded, and I suspect, ill-intended rumour...

"Right fancy writin', i'n't, guv'?" The orderly's presence — and his breath — broke in over Bill's shoulder, but neither penetrated the fury. Bill was outraged! The death, the dirt, the gross incompetence, the distortion of truth, and now what appeared to be a deliberate attempt to deceive the Secretary of State for War.

"'S'matter, guv? Smell got yuh? This 'ere shed's one o' th' better ones. Them what's got walls is worse."

There is much in the condition of Shed Fourteen to anger Bill Lacroix. But what has triggered his conviction that there is collusion to deceive Sidney Herbert?

11

At the Scene of
the Accident

IT WAS THE KIND OF day that Sue Silverberg knew from experience was only going to get worse. The only thing she *wasn't* sure of was just how bad it was going to get, and how soon. This combination of certainty and uncertainty was responsible for her foul mood, and the mood accounted in turn for what she was doing at that moment to a long string of southbound traffic. Highway 50 was one of those busy two-lane thoroughfares that should have been upgraded to four years ago, but never seemed to make the cut whenever budgets got sent back for review.

Sue was driving the big white patrol car at just below the speed limit: too fast to test the courage of drivers behind her; too slow for the anxious heavy-footers who made Highway 50 such a dangerous road.

She looked in the rearview mirror at the growing line of angry drivers. "Serves them right," she grumped to no one in particular, but in saying it, woke up her partner.

Sully Nod was a tribute to his name. He could drop off so

fast in the partner seat that every single member of the force who had ever paired with him swore that he had never actually worked a full shift in his twelve-year career.

"Yeah — aa-*humph*!" Sully had allergies. "Who knows? Maybe with all his lawyers he'll get it put off for another six months."

Sully could wake up as fast as he could fall asleep, but this reply belonged to a conversation that ended five minutes before. It made Sue smile in spite of herself. She even nudged the accelerator a bit. The line behind was getting too long and sooner or later someone was going to try something stupid. One thing about riding with Sully, she thought, it kept you off base, and that went a long way toward healing a lousy mood.

"Maybe," Sue replied, quite willing to revert to the topic that Sully thought was current. It was going to be current with Sue, anyway, for some time, for only a few hours ago she had learned that her upcoming vacation was going to be put on hold by the also-upcoming trial of Charles Xavier Borino, reputed philanthropist and alleged con artist. The case had come forward and been put back at least three times, as Borino's lawyers swarmed at every possible loophole. Sue was a key witness.

Sully was still awake.

"You were going to Vancouver, weren't you," he said. A statement, not a question. There was very little hidden information in Sue's watch.

"Uh-huh." Sue didn't really want to talk about it.

She checked her side mirror and eased into a left turn lane as she slowed for a traffic light at Cedar Mills Blvd.

"Let's get off and go down here a bit," she said. "Let them crank up for a while."

Sully didn't answer. He was asleep again.

The abrupt news of the changed trial date had come on the heels of a transfer notice that really made Sue burn. Of the six people on her regular watch, only Sully and Sindar Mohan were experienced. Now Mohan was being moved, and his replacement was another rookie. Not that rookies are bad in themselves, Sue knew. They have to start somewhere, and traffic is the traditional launch pad. But rookies always seemed to cause so much paperwork. They screwed up more often. Like yesterday. That's why she was on the road with Sully. The kid who was supposed to be behind the wheel today was on sick leave. He'd neglected proper procedure while bringing in a drunk and paid for it with a car door slammed on his fingers.

That meant more paperwork for Sue. Not just the incident itself but all the paper that was piling up on her desk while she was out here doing the kid's job!

That thought stirred up the blackness in her again, but not for long. A snore from Sully crossed a burst of static from the radio.

Sully got to the switch before she did. That happened invariably and it never failed to impress her.

"Aa-*humph*. Twenty-one. Go ahead."

Another burst of static. Sue speeded up to reach a hill for they seemed to be in a reception trough.

"Yeah. Twenty-one. Aa-*humph*. Aa-HUMPH!"

There was a pause at the other end and then a very tentative "Twenty-one? Ah — is your — are you — do you read?"

Sully looked a bit sheepish. "Yes. You've got us. Shoot."

"Okay, twenty-one. We have a call from two-niner-two. Could be a fatality. Cedar Mills Blvd. just west of Number 50. Thought Sergeant Silverberg would want to know."

Sue spoke up. "Thank you, Central. We are only five minutes away."

Sully signed off as Sue made a leaning U-turn to take them back toward and across Highway 50. Two-niner-two was Peterson, the very newest of the rookies. Because the light was green in their favor they made the scene in three minutes.

Sue pulled over to the edge of the road. "I think we need some pictures before anything else" was her first comment.

Sully waved the camera and gave her an I'm-already-there

shake of his head as he got out of the car.

The tableau seemed simple, yet it threw up questions. In fact, it looked like the kind of setup the staff at the police college were so fond of.

On the verge in front of a very well-kept cemetery, facing away from the patrol car, sat a large Mercedes-Benz sedan. It was new — or at least it looked new to Sue. In any case, it was one of those machines that would never have to explain itself.

On the opposite side of the road sat an extremely well-dressed Corvette. Another very noticeable car. And just to make sure, it had a rear bumper sticker that said CATCH ME! One of those machines that got speeding tickets just sitting in the driveway.

What drew the most attention from both of them, however, was the body that had been moved — dragged — from the middle of the road to the cemetery side. It was a dog! Sue looked around the area to make sure she wasn't missing another body — the *real* fatality. Nothing. It was just the dog. One of those strange-looking things that no kid ever has for a pet. Sue had no idea what kind of dog it was, but she could tell you didn't get this one free from the pound.

She went back to the car to turn off the flashers. No sense in attracting gawkers. She did the same for Peterson's patrol car, parked perpendicular to the roadway in the cemetery drive.

Peterson! Where was he, anyway?

Sully apparently had the same thought for he called quietly, "Sue!" and pointed.

At the back of the cemetery, almost out of sight behind a phalanx of headstones, Peterson was bent over, laboriously copying into his notebook.

"Peterson!"

Sue knew she shouldn't have shouted in that tone, but this was too much. There's no way that…

"You! *You!*" Sue was not the only player here with a loud voice. "*You! Policeperson!* You're in charge here, aren't you."

It was a statement. Sue felt that today everybody was making statements to her.

"You'd better be prepared to do something!" The lady was not finished making statements. "Have you any idea what my Fritzie is worth?"

Ah, Sue couldn't help thinking, a question! Even if she didn't have the answer. And somehow she knew she didn't want to know the answer, either. Fritzie had to be the dead dog.

"He's an Entelbucher Sunnehund." The lady was getting louder. "And his real name is Prince's Violet Centaur. Does that mean anything to you?"

Another nonquestion. Sue looked at Sully. What is this today!

"I didn't think it would! It means priceless. That's what it means. Now you…"

Sue tuned out. She was tired of statements. Against her inclination she studied the lady instead of listening. She was of indeterminate age. Could be forty. Could be sixty. Hefty. Hair drawn back. No makeup. Leads with her chin, too, Sue concluded. Probably talks this way even when she isn't upset.

She looked around for skid marks, but couldn't see any. What she did see was Sully, unnecessarily far from the scene, but apparently busy with the camera.

Meanwhile the lady's monologue was interrupted by the hasty arrival of Peterson. He shouted over the lady. "Sergeant Silverberg! Sorry I made Central think it was a fatality, but this lady, she…"

"I said to this young man, now you get…"

"Madam… ma… *madam!*" Sue hated to shout, especially in front of Peterson, but she just had to prevent an instant replay. "Madam, the officer over there will be in charge of this investigation." She pointed at Sully, who was getting farther and farther away. "Constable Nod. Give your statement to him. And, madam, make sure you give him all the details. Now, Peterson…"

Sue turned and took the young policeman with her before

the lady could wind up again. "Now, Peterson," she repeated.

"I just came on the scene, Sergeant. I'm patroling Cedar Mills going east, see…"

Sue had a sinking feeling; yet she kept silent. Somehow this case was taking on the odor of complication — and paperwork. If she was careful there might be a way around that.

"… and I saw this body — well, the dog — in the road. And the big one, the MB, was here, see, and over there was the 'Vette."

For the first time, Marv glanced at the drivers. The man in the Mercedes was sitting in the front seat, looking studiously bored. The Corvette driver was leaning on the fender of her vehicle. She was very young. A kid, really. She was trying to look bored.

"This was how long ago?" Sue asked.

Peterson looked at his watch. "Thirty-four minutes now." He added proudly, "I arrived on the scene at 8:56."

"Okay. Okay. Then what?"

"Anyway, I saw it was only a dog, but I got some pictures."

Sue was pleased at that.

"And I pulled the dog to the side. No point in blocking traffic, right? But here's the fix."

Peterson had his notepad out and held up in front of him almost as though he were testifying.

"The kid, the girl with the 'Vette — it's hers, by the way — she says she's been in the cemetery for nearly an hour. Got a local history project in school so she's in the back there getting names and dates off the stones. See? I wrote down the ones she said. Now, the girl says she heard tires, not real loud, then a *thunk*. She looked up and saw the guy in the MB stopped in the middle of the road and then pulled over. When the kid got to the road she saw the dog. It twitched a bit, then stopped.

"Now, I got here only a few minutes later, and the story I got — I talked to the MB guy first — is that he, the MB guy, and

At the Scene of the Accident

the kid were coming down the road toward each other and *the kid hit the dog!* Then the kid did a U-ey. Like she was going to run? But then she changed her mind and pulled over.

"And then this lady! What a stirfry! Anyway, it's her dog. A champion of something. Did you know it's a —" Peterson read from his notes "En — tell-buck-er-sen."

"Yeah, I got that, Peterson." Sue didn't want the rookie making statements, too. "What did you do then?"

"Well, I told the drivers to go to their cars. Got to get everyone away from this lady. Then I called Central. First I checked the front of the cars. Both bumpers are clean — you can see for yourself. Meantime, the lady took off to call her lawyer. So the only thing I think I've got to do till you get here is check the kid's story. That's why I was back there when you came."

Sue knew for sure now that the day was already worse. In point of fact, it was now a matter of whether the whole year was going to go sour. This case seemed likely to turn into a lawsuit. She took a breath very slowly and held it.

"What *else* did you do then, Peterson?"

"Why... nothing. What else is there?"

Sue Silverberg just groaned.

Someone has finally asked Sue Silverberg a question, a clear question, but it makes her groan. What has the rookie Peterson neglected to do that would go a long way to resolving the opposing stories of the two drivers?

12

The Midterm Exam: Which Way Is Up?

THE SUDDEN APPEARANCE OF AN image on the huge drop screen reduced the buzz of conversation in the auditorium to whispers as soon as Professor Sean Hennigar turned on the overhead projector. Latecomers rushed for the few remaining seats near the front. A few of them despaired of finding an empty chair, and simply hunched on the floor of the center aisle.

"As you were told in the opening lecture of the course —" Sean began. The silence now was absolute; he never spoke very loud at any time and the opening sentences of his lectures were especially soft; it was his technique for filling the front rows and getting instant attention when he started, "— for a passing grade, you will be required to interpret a representation, or 'map.' The 'map' is what you now see before you on the screen."

A single tardy student clumping in through the upper rear doors was scowled into a tiptoeing crouch when the entire back row of students turned simultaneously. In today's class there was no time for nonsense or interruption. This was the midterm exam. It was one of the two occasions each term (the other being the final exam) when attendance was perfect and attention was absolute for the once-a-week lecture in Adventures in Archaeology 333.

The reality was that not many students took "AA-cubed," as they called it, very seriously at first, for neither Scan nor his co-instructor, Professor Swift, had illusions that the course was anything but a science course specifically designed and modified for nonscience students. "Bird science" was the generic title given courses like this one, a title that did not have the slightest connection with ornithology.

Years before, the Senate of the university had earnestly decreed the necessity of science for arts students and required therefore that all "artsies" pass a minimum of one such course in order to graduate. Junior faculty invariably were stuck with these students, few of whom could tell a quadratic equation from a test tube, or even, as the chair of Physical Sciences once put it, use a calculator right side up. The result was courses like "Amazing Physics," "Tabletop Chemistry" and the surprisingly popular "Adventures in Archaeology," taught by Sean and Dr. MaryPat Swift. One of the reasons for its popularity was the style of examination the two instructors dreamed up each year: bizarre on the surface, and certainly in the mode of *Raiders of the Lost Ark*, these exams were nevertheless a serious challenge in thinking, and a breath of fresh air to students accustomed to the tedium of instructors who saw science only as SCIENCE.

"Your challenge," Sean said, continuing his explanation, "is to choose the proper *aspect* by which to interpret this representation."

He took a pen from somewhere in the folds of his tattered poncho, which instead of an academic gown was his regular and constant lecturing attire. (Whether he actually wore a shirt underneath it was a subject of considerable discussion in the campus pub.)

"You have no doubt noticed on the screen," he said, tracing

the outline of the figure on the transparency with the pen's sharp point, "what appears to be a large letter H."

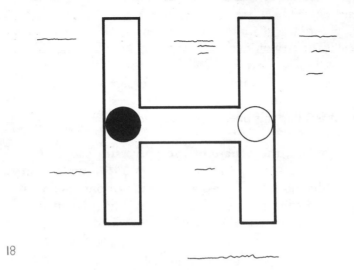

18

Indeed, the image did look like a large H outlined in black. Both vertical bars and the horizontal bar were drawn faithfully straight and in the proportions of the Western alphabet's eighth letter. The three bars were only about the width of Sean's thumb on the transparency, but projected on the screen, they appeared much wider.

In every way the image looked just like an ordinary letter H, except that from where the students sat, the outline of a circle filled the intersection of the horizontal bar and the right vertical. An identical circle, but solid — shaded in — filled the intersection on the opposite side. In the lower left corner, somewhat fainter than the rest of the diagram, was the number 18. At several intermittent points, below, on and above the H, were even fainter marks, indistinguishable, but clearly in a regular horizontal pattern.

"Your assumptions are as follows." Sean looked out at the

56

class. "One, that this is an *old map* locating an object of supreme religious significance to a distant, somewhat primitive mountain culture, probably the Salubrian, or it could be the Egregian. That won't be an important difference until your final exam with Dr. Swift. For now, all you need to deal with is that the map is from one culture or the other."

At the mention of MaryPat Swift, there was a general rustle, and grins. Professor Swift was an acknowledged rebel on the faculty. A full professor, tenured because of her extensive publications, she was unlike senior staff in that she deliberately taught at least one bird science course a term. Part of student lore on the campus was her alleged practice of taking a bag of birdseed, not to her lectures, but to meetings of the science department! MaryPat shared the teaching of "AA-cubed" with Sean.

"*Two*" — Sean tapped the transparency with his pen "— the map was recently found in a book that has been in storage at the British Museum for the past hundred and fifty years or so. And *three*, the parallel bars represent vertical shafts dug in the earth. If you dig down one of them, you will locate this treasured religious object. It is represented by the shaded-in circle. The other circle — the one in outline — is a highly sensitive and destructive booby trap. Obviously you don't want to dig into that one.

"For a passing grade then, you must choose the proper aspect of this map. That is, identify the *top* and bottom so that you'll dig — theoretically, of course — down the correct shaft. There are four possible views. One is correct. Don't forget to explain your reasoning. Remember that no respectable archaeologist would take a chance on being only half certain, because of the booby trap. Those of you who wish to come forward and examine either the screen or the transparency more closely may do so.

"May I remind you that this question constitutes one-half of your grade. The other half may be earned in the final examination, which Dr. Swift will present in the last class. Are there any questions?"

Would you get a passing grade? What are the four possible views of this map and which is the correct one? (For the other half of your mark, go to Dr. Swift's exam next, in The Final Exam: Digging in the Right Place.*)*

13

The Final Exam: Digging in the Right Place*

FINAL EXAMINATION
Adventures in Archaeology 333

27 April, A.M.   Lecture Hall A/B/C
Examiner: MaryPat Swift, B.A., Dip.C.S.,
M.Sc., LL.D. (Paris)

NOTE: Candidates are reminded that results of this examination constitute one-half of their total grade. Those candidates who did not achieve a passing grade in the midterm examination are nevertheless eligible to sit for this final.
M.P.S.

You have been given a map, which shows a buried object of supreme religious signifcance to a culture that you have determined to be either Salubrian or Egregian. The distinction may eventually be important since in the Salubrian culture all religious ceremonies are performed with the participants

*Before attempting this five-minute mystery, be sure to solve the previous one: *The Midterm Exam: Which Way Is Up?*

facing south, whereas the Egregians do the exact opposite.

The map is in the form of a letter H. One vertical arm represents a shaft dug in the earth to bury this object. The other leads to a sensitive booby trap. If you have determined which shaft is the safe and which the dangerous one (by completing the midterm examination successfully) you are ready for the excavation. Your task now involves decisions about this excavation.

Here are the details:

Having received a sizable research grant, you have been able to travel to the upper reaches of Salubria (actually, of what you *think* is Salubria; it's very poorly charted) to do a trial excavation. Regrettably, travel being what it is in that part of the world, you and your somewhat unreliable guide have had a difficult time. By car, muleback and finally on foot, through tunnels and over badly mapped mountain passes, you have come to what you believe is the Salubrian plain, on the border of Egregia.

During this arduous trek, you are aware that you crossed and recrossed the border of the two countries several times, and suspect that you crossed it several more times without knowing it. You don't know with any certainty whether you are in Salubria now or just outside it in Egregia.

Moments ago, you emerged from yet another tunnel to see before you the clear evidence of two shafts dug in the earth, some eight to ten meters apart, just as your "map" shows. Between them stands an adult Salubrian. At least, it *may* be a Salubrian; it could just as easily be an Egregian, because there is nothing in their appearance that would enable you to tell them apart.

To complicate your situation, an exact duplication of this scene can be detected off in the distance. There, just out of range of a shout, is another pair of shafts, eight to ten meters apart, with an Egregian — or is it a Salubrian? — standing between them.

Precisely at midpoint between the two sites is a tall pole. You can see it from where you stand, bisecting the setting sun. Hanging limply at the top in the windless dusk are both a Salubrian and an Egregian flag. You are on the border, all right, but which country is which?

One good result has come from your advance research. You know that in the Salubrian culture, truth is the primary value of daily life and the essential element for redemption, so that Salubrians can always be counted on to tell the truth. Egregians are exactly the opposite. Lying is, for them, the ultimate art form and spiritual realization.

There are three requirements for the successful completion of this examination: One, *you must approach* either *but* not both *of the two subjects you see.* Two, *you may then ask the Salubrian or the Egregian, as the case may be, a* single *question to find out where you are.* Three, *you must then describe in a short paragraph what your digging strategy will be.*

Could you pass this examination?

14

A Double Assassination
at "The Falls"

OUT OF HABIT, VINCE MORO reached up to clean a finger-print off the rearview mirror, before adjusting it down a bit so he could see out the back. Then he picked up the envelope that was balled up and stuffed behind the gearshift in the center console, and put it in the glove compartment.

Don't know why I'm doing this, Vince thought as he reach-ed over to pick up a pair of cigarette butts from the floor on the passenger side. "I really don't know why." This time he said it out loud, while throwing the two butts out the passenger side window — or what was left of it.

The fact was, Vince was compulsively neat, and nothing bothered him more than a messy car. It was a point of personal pride that no vehicle left Vince's Auto Body dirty. Not ever, no matter how tiny or insignificant the repair.

But this car? There was surely no point in cleaning it. Certainly no point in trying to repair it. The thing was a write-off, and Vince was simply here to tow it away to the wrecking yard. The front and back of the car were okay. In fact, the dash had that spotless, uncluttered look Vince always liked in cars that had just left a rental agency. And the shelf beneath the back window was pleasantly free of the invariable accumulation of clutter and junk.

The front seats, however, and the front windows, the center post, even the roof above the front seat: they were a different matter. The killers had sprayed so many bullets over these areas that the headrest on the passenger seat had been chewed right off, leaving a frothy stump of stuffing, its original whiteness now covered in drying blood. A few minutes ago Vince had overheard one of the investigators — he was sure it was one of the CIA guys — say that both victims had taken over twenty rounds in the upper torso.

"You the guy from Hertz?"

The voice in Vince's ear startled him, but he strove not to show it. His hearing more than his sight told him it was the sergeant from the highway patrol. Although the two men had met before, more than once, the sergeant never, ever recognized Vince. Or pretended not to. Vince didn't like him.

"I have been *retained* by Hertz," Vince said, getting out of the car with deliberate slowness. "I'm here to take the car. It's cleared to go?"

He folded his arms and leaned against the car. It was the same sergeant all right. A tall fellow, at least a head taller than Vince. And he had the annoying habit of standing so close when he talked that the other person had to lean back to look up, or else step backward. That's why Vince leaned against the car.

"Not yet," the sergeant replied as he took off his hat and wiped his forehead with his sleeve. Vince was sure he was actually moving closer.

"Not yet," the policeman said again. "There has to be some —"

"Okay, Sergeant, if you will, please! The photographer can use you now."

Vince whipped around quickly. It was not a voice he'd

heard before, today or at any time. The accent was British, and as the speaker approached, Vince knew he was a complete stranger. That was not surprising; the place was crawling with investigators. The CIA was here; Vince knew that for sure. And the RCMP. Two of them had come from Ottawa in a Lear jet. And the whole scene had been shut down while they waited for two more people to come up from Buffalo. No one had told Vince directly, but he could tell they were in charge. Now who the British guy was, Vince had no idea at all, but certainly he was connected with the affair.

Just before dawn, two diplomats from the French consulate in Buffalo, New York, had crossed into Canada over the Rainbow Bridge at Niagara Falls. Not more than a few minutes later, while stopped at a traffic light, they were shot down in an absolute storm of machine-gun bullets. Then their bodies had been dragged out of the car and, as though to send a message, laid side by side in front of the car and sprayed with bullets again. The assassins had escaped.

"Excuse me, sir." The British accent was very polite. A great deal more polite than the sergeant. "Who are... oh, yes. Forgive me!"

The man peered closer at the badge that dangled from Vince's shirt pocket and proclaimed CLEARANCE – SITE ONLY.

"You're the gentleman here to tow away the vehicle, aren't you? If you don't mind waiting just a few minutes more. Some photos we need. It would be convenient if you didn't drive over the outlines there."

He pointed to the chalk outlines on the pavement in front of the car, which marked where the bodies of the diplomats had lain. The sergeant was now lying down beside the longer one. It was clear his dignity was wounded and Vince was just beginning to enjoy that when the accent said, "There's one more thing, actually. It's frightfully awkward, I know, but you... uh... you are just about the size of one of the victims. Do you... uh... would you mind awfully lying down there like the sergeant? I'm sorry, I can't really explain why, but it will help us. A reconstruct-the-scene sort of thing, you see."

For an instant, but only an instant, Vince wondered if maybe he wasn't being had. But the sergeant was already lying on the pavement, and the situation was hardly one for humor, macabre or otherwise. He nodded and went to the front of the car, glad now that he'd left on his coveralls to drive out here, and lay down beside the other outline.

"A bit embarrassing, this," Vince muttered to the sergeant. There was no response. The sergeant was definitely embarrassed and had no wish to discuss the fact. "All in the interests of justice," Vince continued, determined to make it known that he could make light of the indignity. "By the way," he said, "would it help if you knew which one of them was driving when they were shot?"

The sergeant sat bolt upright so suddenly that the photographer yelled. "How do you know?" the policeman asked.

How does Vince Moro know who was driving?

65

15

They Come in Threes, Don't They?

THE DOOR TO THE INNER office opened quietly, but Mike Dunn didn't pay much attention. He and his wife, Dale, had run Dunn & Dunn Insurance Brokers together for so long now that they could interpret each other's purpose much of the time without exchanging a word. In this particular instance Mike's subconscious told him that the way the door had opened signaled no more than "errand: no communication necessary." Dale had something to pick up or look up or enter in a file: something that couldn't be done in her own office.

Nevertheless, this errand got his attention. Dale had the morning paper and on her way to the file cabinet quietly set it on the corner of Mike's desk.

The headline announced
CASTRO SCOOPS UP REST OF SUGAR INDUSTRY.

Mike stared at it for a long time, unwilling to look directly at his wife. When he finally did, she was smiling at him gently. After the briefest of pauses, he smiled back and said,

"Thanks. It would have been easy to say 'I told you so.'"

Dale just shrugged. "No milk was spilt," she said, then changed the subject immediately to show she meant it. "Have you looked at the applications that came in this morning?" she asked.

"Right here," Mike replied, glad for the shift away from anything to do with Cuba. "Go through them yourself. See what you think. I like the guy from New Denmark. He's even got — now where is it? — ah, here! His résumé is the only one with a title page. Lends a little class, I thought."

He handed the résumé to Dale. It was in an acetate folder and the front page read:

R. David Sloan
12 Colonial Street
New Denmark, Ontario

Tel. No.,
Quaker 4 - 7124

D.O.B.,
31 May 1932

Present Employer,
Islington Insurance Agency

"Looks organized, doesn't he?" Mike enthused. "At least from the appearance of that. And if we are going to have an office way out in Rexdale, one of the first things we need is someone who is organized, don't you agree? By the way, you don't think Islington would say we stole him, do you? I wouldn't want —"

The ring of the telephone stopped him short. That was another part of the accustomed practice between him and Dale. It was a given in the office that most of the time, a telephone call meant a client call, and that took immediate precedence. At home it was always a contest to see who could outwait the other in picking up the receiver, but not here.

"Dunn and Dunn," Mike said into the receiver.

"Mikey boy!" the caller began. Mike Dunn knew instantly who it was. With a curl of distaste on his lips he looked up at Dale and mouthed, "Mac, at the service station." With his free hand he made a revolver sign at the telephone and pulled the trigger.

"Hello, Mac. What did you find?"

"Mikey! You feedin' this thing Purina maybe, 'stead of Texaco? Don't blame yuh! Yuh've gotta feed dog food to a dog!" He burst into a loud cackle at his own joke, as Mike's heart sank.

"Just how bad is it?" he asked.

"Well, Mikey, I got the fuel pump fixed. Stopped the leak, anyways. And the hood's unstuck now. But those automatic transmission buttons. I mean — it's nuts puttin' them in the center of the steering wheel! Look, I gotta take the steering column right out — the *whole steering column*! You're looking at another six, maybe eight hours' labor."

Mike sat silently, his forehead now cupped in the revolver hand.

"Hey, Mikey! You still there, boy?"

"That's *two!*" Mike said.

"What? Two what? What're yuh talkin' about?"

"Nothing." Mike sat up straight and cleared his throat. "Mac, don't touch the thing till I call you back, okay? I've got to think about this. I just may write it off."

"Your car, Mikey boy. Whatever you say. But listen, I gotta bill yuh for…"

"I know, I know." Mike cut him off. "Of course you do. I'll call you back before noon," he said, and hung up.

For a moment, silence hung heavy in the office, until Dale asked, "What *is* 'two,' anyway?"

There was silence for still another moment as Mike teetered on the edge of anger and self-recrimination, but gradually his innate good humor took over.

"You're the two," he said to his wife. "Number *one* is, you said not to buy one of those new Edsels last year. And how right you were! Mac practically owns us now. *Two* is right here." He pointed at the morning paper. "You said to sell our shares in Bowman Sugar when that fellow Castro took over in Cuba this summer, because he'd nationalize everything. I didn't agree but... thank heavens we did!"

Dale frowned just a little. "I'm not completely with you here. So we won one and lost one. We sold the sugar stock and we bought an Edsel. Maybe we should keep it. The thing's so bad it could be valuable someday! What I don't get is the *one, two!*"

Mike looked up at her. "*Threes*, Dale," he said. "Everything comes in threes, doesn't it? Now, you've been bang on twice already this morning. I'm just wondering what the third is going to be!"

Dale opened her mouth then closed it again, but not before Mike reacted. "Oh, no!" he said. "The third?"

Dale just nodded, then said, "Here. R. David Sloan."

What about R. David Sloan troubles Dale?

16

Witness to a Hit-and-Run

DIANE VAN HOOF GLANCED AT her watch. Five more minutes. That's when the mysterious caller — she'd called herself "Betty" — said she'd be here.

"I seen d'car what hit 'er," she'd said in that pinched-lip style that Diane had now become so used to hearing. "I'll tell yuz what I seen." (*H'oil tell yuz whud hoi seen.*) "But not on d'phone. D'Two Seasons. In d'café dere."

They had agreed on a time, and that's why Diane now sat on one of the hard wooden chairs in the lobby café of the Two Seasons Motor Hotel. The name of the place was typical of the ironic humor one encountered here in Labrador, particularly in the northern part, where humor was almost the only defence against the bleakness and — for anybody from "The South" — the overpowering sense of isolation.

Diane was from "The South," a local expression that, for all practical purposes, meant the rest of the world. There was no "north"; *they were the north!* And if there was an "east" or a "west," Diane hadn't heard of them yet. Only The South.

She nodded gratefully at the young waiter as he adjusted the blinds, having noticed that the sun was shining directly into her face. At the same time she couldn't help being a cop, and made careful note of how out of place the young man looked in this plaid-shirt, macho mining town, with his sallow, indoors complexion setting off the hair tied back in a ponytail.

Diane wanted to tell him to turn down the thermostat too. That was another thing she'd noticed right away, as soon as the RCMP had transferred her to Labrador. All the buildings were overheated. It was as though the idea was to cook away winter, which was by far the longer of Labrador's "two seasons."

At the training college in Regina, there'd been only one lecture on acclimatization, the art of adjusting to a new post. This was Diane's second full-time assignment in her seven-year career. She'd now had enough experience to confirm for her that more than one lecture was needed to prepare police officers for the little things.

Her first assignment had been with the drug squad in Windsor, and although she'd been well trained for the antidrug detail, no one had really warned her about the impact of working across the river from crime-ridden Detroit. Now Labrador. She'd been ready for the cold and for the isolation, but nobody had told her she'd have to oversee the spray-painting of giant snowbanks along the runways at the airport, so that pilots without radar could find it on sunny days when reflection made them blind.

And no one had told her how meaningless the restaurant menus would be by midwinter. Most of their food came from "The South," and if the fall stockup was miscalculated or the weather was bad enough to preclude air-freighted fresh food (at shocking prices), then the only certainty was caribou: caribou steak, caribou stew, caribou burger... One of the latter was sitting heavily in her stomach right now, the only item on the luncheon menu that the kitchen could fill.

"You be's d'new constable d'en?"

Diane started. For an instant, the memory of another lecture flashed across her mind: the one about the danger of daydreaming in uniform in a public place.

She stood up, embarrassed, and offered her hand. "You're Betty? Constable Diane Van Hoof." Betty was confused for a moment, then took the offered hand limply.

"Please sit down," Diane said. "Would you like some coffee? Tea?"

Betty nodded. "Sure. (*Shore.*) D'tea." She sat down opposite Diane. In her enormous parka, which was still tightly zipped, she overflowed the chair like a bundle of freight on a loading dock.

"I seen 'im 'it 'er. Blue Jimmy. Jus' like ours." (*Arz.*) "I can't stay long. Me 'usband'll be 'ome soon. 'E's in d'mine." (*D'moine.*) "Likes 'is meal quick when 'e gits 'ome. 'E said to phone yuz."

All this came out in a rapid burst that entirely belied Betty's behavior. She seemed slow, lethargic. Her appearance suggested that, and on the telephone her voice had, too. But now she seemed tense, very hyper.

The issue was a hit-and-run accident two days earlier that had the town in an uproar. A native child had been struck down on the road not far from the community school. The driver and the vehicle had disappeared. There were absolutely no clues, and until now, no witnesses. The child had been airlifted south and now hovered between life and death in a Montreal hospital. Diane knew that if the little girl died, the racial tensions that regularly simmered beneath the surface here could well blow up into a major problem. As it was, the potential for trouble was high no matter what the outcome.

"We lives near d'school." Betty was obviously not given to small talk or long preambles. "I'm settin' out d'supper and I hears a bump 'n' I looks out 'n' dere's d'kid lyin' dere. And she's a blue Jimmy drivin' away."

Despite the excitement of a possible breakthrough on this hit-and-run case, Diane couldn't suppress her fascination at how, by pinching her mouth forward at both edges, Betty could talk almost without moving her lips.

"Me 'usband said to tell yuz. 'E said to tell yuz, too, we don't want nothin' t'do with no court. 'Specially now he works d'swing fer a while startin' next week. But see, we's got one a' dem Jimmys, too. She's black. 'F anybody else seen it — d'kid, I mean — we don't want no mixup, me 'usband said."

Betty had unzipped her coat finally to take out a package of cigarettes. For the first time, Diane noticed the tobacco stains on the woman's fingers, then in a few seconds understood why. As soon as Betty lit up, she began reflexively flicking the filtered end with her thumb, holding the coal more or less over the ash tray.

Diane really wasn't sure how to approach the next stage. It was obvious Betty's message was complete, for she sat in silence, sipping tea with one hand and flicking the cigarette with the other, alternating sips with drags.

She decided on the direct approach. "It's very good of you to come forward. Now, of course, I'm going to have to talk to your husband, too. Then I'll have to see your Jimmy." She took out her notebook. "We're talking about a General Motors vehicle, right? The Jimmy? Does your husband drive it to work regularly?"

For an instant — only an instant — the teacup stopped en route to Betty's lips while she flicked furiously on the cigarette end. It wasn't much, but it was the confirmation Diane was looking for. She knew now she'd have to push even harder.

Specifically, what makes Diane Van Hoof suspicious of Betty's account of the hit-and-run accident?

17

The Plot at the Rockface

ON THE EASTERN FACE OF the mountain, up very, very high, the six men toiled numbly, side by side. Had he bothered to go to the extreme southeastern corner of the compound and look up (which he never did), the commandant would have been able to just make out the six tiny figures with their guard. He would not have been able to see exactly what it was they were working at, but, then, he didn't need to. He knew.

The labor was backbreaking. As each man heaved and swung his sledgehammer he would grunt, as though a hammer could never connect with the rockface unless pushed there by the expulsion of air through the larynx. The men's bodies shuddered with each blow on the unyielding rock. *Thunk! thunk thunk thunk! thunk-a-thunk! Thunk!* There was no rhythm. Just lift. Then smash. Try to lift again. *Thunk!* Hang on till the next break. There would be water to drink. Then the tongues that felt like dead tree branches would cool, and shrink enough for easier breathing.

Most of the time the hammers just bounced off the rock.

Then every once in a while a crack would appear, a hairline. More pounding. The crack would open and become a fissure. Still more pounding. Finally a piece would break off and fall to the narrow platform at their feet. When there were enough of these, the guard would tap the barrel of his rifle against the water bucket: the signal to load the wheelbarrows and wrestle them down along the narrow winding ledge to dump the pieces into the gorge below so that more men could pound these pieces into smaller pieces. From there the pieces went into dilapidated coal cars and were freighted — no one really knew where. Down to the coast, that much the prisoners knew. Probably all the way to Dubrovnik.

Negotiating the wheelbarrows down the twisting ledge was easier than the pounding, but much more dangerous. A wrong step and it was over the edge, straight down to certain death. Even if only the wheelbarrow slipped over, it was the end for whoever had been pushing it. The barrow could not be retrieved, so the Romanian guards simply stood the prisoner on the spot where it had gone over and gave him a choice: jump or be pushed.

Just yesterday it had happened again, and the prisoner had jumped. He even gave the guards the finger first, but no one from the work party on the rockface believed the guards understood the gesture. They were too stupid.

Certainly the one they called Igor was. A foul-smelling brute with a lower lip that drooped so far it obscured most of his chin. He had an incredibly hairy face, which even the fanatical SS officer assigned to the camp could never get the man to shave. None of the prisoners had the faintest idea what Igor's real name might be. No one wanted to know. A name personalizes. Makes connections that in turn make it harder to hate. Or kill.

Igor tapped the bucket. The six men dropped their hammers and moved to the wheelbarrows with the stooped, robotlike movement that humans acquire when their lives are being crushed by mindless, exhausting labor. Except for one very tall man. He walked a little straighter — but not too much straighter. He was very careful not to draw unnecessary attention to himself. But clearly he was not as deadened as the rest.

That's because he had joined the group only this morning to bring the complement back up to six. The Romanian guards and their SS adviser knew him as Vlad Kljuc (number 475216), a partisan and a Communist from somewhere here in the republic of Montenegro. His real name was Trevor Hawkes, and he was formerly a machinist from Bristol, and now a member of His Majesty's Special Air Service, the SAS. Just prior to his "capture," he had graduated from the Allies' mysterious Camp X outside Toronto, in Canada.

Trevor Hawkes was here for one purpose only: to free and bring to Dubrovnik, by any means possible, one Peter Nova, the man now walking just ahead of him toward the wheelbarrows. Nova, Trevor knew (and it was all he knew), was a Slovene from Ljubljanca, who had a reputation in the Yugoslavian resistance as the one Communist leader who wanted to bring Communist and royalist factions together peacefully. He had been teaching at the University of Zagreb until 1941, when the Nazis had moved into Yugoslavia. Two years later they scooped up all the known Communists at the university and brought them up here to the camp on Kuk. Now the Allies wanted Nova badly. Trevor Hawkes had no idea why, but that was the least of his concerns right now. Right now he was simply following Peter Nova, waiting for an opportunity to do more talking.

The trip with the wheelbarrows was free of incident, and when Igor brought them all back to the rockface he signaled a rest, waiting in slow-witted anticipation for what he'd seen happen every single time before. It happened again.

The six men who had worked side by side with the hammers on the narrow and dangerous little ledge, and who followed one another carefully and silently to the dumping site, now sat three against three like adversaries. Which, indeed, is what they were.

The SS adviser — no fool — insisted that every work party must number six: three Communists, followers of the partisan Josip Tito, and three royalists, Draza Mihajlovic's men. Left alone and rested, they were as likely to set on one another as on their Axis captors.

Until three months ago the two sides, royalist and Communist, had put aside their differences, albeit uneasily, to face the common enemy. But now, in spite of the efforts of leaders like Peter Nova, their civil war was open and vicious, with their respective forces often trying to go around the Axis occupiers to get at one another. This kind of passion, properly used, made camp control a lot easier. Facing Trevor and Nova, therefore, were three Serbian royalists — two farmers and a civil servant from Belgrade.

"So just *how* do you propose to accomplish this dramatic scheme?" Nova looked straight ahead as he spit the words at Trevor.

For the big SAS man the question was a breakthrough, despite the acrimony in the tone. Until this morning Nova had had no idea who Trevor was, and certainly didn't know that his capture was really a deliberate insertion. But the question meant Trevor had been accepted now, however warily. What had tipped the balance was Trevor's having mentioned, during the previous rest, some very private, personal facts that had been supplied by Nova's sister. So far so good. Now he had to get the wiry little man to agree to an escape attempt.

"The basket," Trevor replied, leaning forward to massage his ankles.

"The basket? Go out in the basket? You're a fool!" Nova hissed loudly, then realized he had attracted Igor's attention. His face turned very serious. He pointed to the wheelbarrows and spoke to Igor in Serb.

"Your wife has just given birth to pigs again."

The royalists were suddenly alert. None of them looked up, but one smiled a little. As for Igor, it was obvious he couldn't follow. He looked back and forth from Nova to the wheelbarrows as a string of drool slipped over the edge of his ponderous lower lip, heading for his waist. He waved the rifle barrel in a dismissive gesture. It broke the string.

"Either you're an idiot or you think I am." Nova was talking to Trevor again. "It won't work in the first place, because you need *two* men to get the basket across. One can't pull it up. It won't hold three and I won't leave *him!*" Nova pointed with his eyes at the man on his right, the third of the Communist trio, then added, in an almost defeated way, "Those three over there will cut his throat the instant they've got him alone."

Trevor's reply unnerved Nova. "I know," he said.

With a jerk of his head, Igor seemed to remember why they were there and tapped the water bucket. Rest was over. So was dialogue. At the next break, their rations were brought up by two other guards. In their presence no one dared to break the rule of silence, for these two had a leg up on Igor, and it wasn't until after the first trip down the ledge with the wheelbarrows that Trevor could continue.

"We all go. The royals, too. All six of us," he said.

"*In the basket?*" Nova still didn't believe Trevor. "*All* of us? I suppose two at a time and your real name is Noah!"

The "basket" was a means of transport across the deep valley that local inhabitants had devised, who knows how many years before. It was a rope-and-pulley affair, with one terminus just up the path from the rockface where the six men were working. Its power was human strength. Two adults — all it would hold — were needed to pull it across to the other side because of the upward angle. At that terminus, another narrow pathway snaked up for a short distance to a pass and then disappeared. The return to this side needed only one person. The basket rolled back most of the way, but its weight caused the rope to sag so that from about fifty feet out, it needed a passenger to pull it in the rest of the way.

The SS officer had ordered it cut down, but because he never came up here, and because the Romanian guards were mountain people and liked to amuse themselves with it, the basket still hung there, a tantalizing sight to those prisoners who dared glance up the path to look at it. Even so, there had never been a single escape from the camp, via the basket or by any other method, because of the trackless mountain wilderness, sure death to anyone who didn't know where — or how — to go.

Trevor was unruffled by Nova's objections. "I have a way," he said.

Nova was silent for a minute. "What about Igor? I suppose you're going to —"

His sentence stopped there as he followed Trevor's gaze to the hammers. But now his tone changed from one of petulant objection to simple skepticism.

"The royalists," he continued, raising his chin at the three, who were, as usual, ranged opposite. "What if they don't want to go? Or if they want to go some other way?"

Trevor looked straight at Nova for the first time. "Do you think they'd want to stay and explain what happened to Igor? And there's only one other way out if they stay on this side, and that's back down through camp. Unless they're mountain climbers, and they don't look like it to me."

Now Nova was really interested.

"When would we go?" he wanted to know.

"First time there's fog. My guess is tomorrow morning. We should have gone today! It would have been perfect!"

"But then..."

Nova's next objection was anticipated. "I know the way." Trevor said. "That's why I'm here. We go to Dubrovnik. You'll be met there. It's tricky, but I've been a climber for years. I can get us down if you do what I say. All that's needed now is for you to explain to them."

Peter Nova stared at the ground for just a moment. His nostrils flared slightly as he took a deep breath. Then he began to speak to Igor in Serb, all the while pointing to his shoes, then pulling up his pantleg and flapping it in a demonstration for the puzzled guard.

"You three," he said. "Listen to me. We're getting out. Escaping. All of us. The new one here... *don't look at me! Look at the guard!* Now hear me out."

Igor's gaze followed Nova's pointing from shoe to pantleg and back again. However he interpreted it, he didn't like it, and tapped the water bucket.

Nova concluded with "I'll say more next rest period."

Had Igor been any brighter he might have noticed a new animation in the step of his work party as they filed back to the rockface. Even the third Communist, who had not been able to hear all of Trevor's presentation and who could not speak Serb, seemed to be infected by a sense that something was up.

The mood almost cracked at the next and last break. There was another problem.

"It still won't work," Nova said to Trevor. "Even if the royalists cooperate, we just can't let ourselves be outnumbered. Either this side or over there. Feelings are too deep. They'll slit our throats."

Trevor's calm never shifted. "I've thought of that, too," he said.

What is Trevor Hawkes's plan for getting the two sets of enemies across the deep valley, given all the problems Peter Nova has brought up?

18

Regina Versus Kirk

12 March

Memo to Wm. Seeley,
        c/o Seeley, Leeballoux, & Trace

From Nat Neffer Transcription Services

Regarding **Regina Versus Kirk**

Bill,

Attached is a copy of the transcript from Day 2, as you requested (minus pages 18 through 20). I have not included Judge Benoit's opening caution to the jury because it's word for word, as on Day 1.

    I apologize again for the missing pages at the end. That's when the machine broke, as I told you on the phone. It should be up and running tomorrow and I'll fax the rest to you ASAP.

Gloria

BENOÎT: Call your next witness, Mr. Ford.

FORD: The Crown calls Dr. Finlay J. Quinn.

(Quinn sworn in)

FORD: Please state your name and occupation for the record.

QUINN: Finlay J. Quinn, doctor of forensic pathology in private practice.

FORD: Dr. Quinn, did you attend at the death of Thorvald Heintzmann, on request of the Bayview Homicide Division?

QUINN: Yes.

FORD: Is this your report of findings?

QUINN: Yes.

FORD: Your Honor, the Crown wishes to enter Dr. Quinn's pathology report as an exhibit.

(Report entered as Exhibit A)

FORD: Now, Dr. Quinn, could you tell the court what you established as the time and cause of death?

QUINN: Using accepted forensic procedures, and given that I was able to attend fairly shortly after the shooting, I was able to determine that death occurred between 4:45 and 5:15 P.M. on July 14 of last year. The victim died of three gunshot wounds to the chest. They were fired from a .25 caliber weapon, and all three bullets passed through the body. The spent bullets lay on the floor by the south wall of the room.

FORD: They didn't lodge in the wall?

QUINN: No. It's not likely that shells of that caliber would have enough remaining force to do so after passing through an adult chest.

FORD: For the bullets to pass through the body then, the person shooting would have to be standing fairly close?

QUINN: Within six or seven feet, in my opinion.

FORD: Was death instant?

QUINN: Within one to three minutes in my opinion.

FORD: That's all I have, Your Honor.

BENOÎT: Mr. Seeley?

SEELEY: Dr. Quinn, these three gunshot wounds, were they grouped on Mr. Heintzmann's chest?

QUINN: Grouped?

SEELEY: Close together.

QUINN: One shot went in directly below the sternum. Brushed it. Another was about five inches to the left and up forty-five degrees. The third was three inches below that... sort of at seven o'clock from the second wound. The precise measurements are in my report. There's a diagram, too.

SEELEY: Is it possible to tell which one was the most effective killing shot?

QUINN: Yes. The third one I mentioned. It did the most damage to the heart.

SEELEY: And it was the third one fired?

QUINN: That's not possible to tell for certain.

SEELEY: So that particular shot could have been the second or even the first one fired.

QUINN: Yes.

SEELEY: Thank you. No more.

BENOÎT: If there's no redirect, Mr. Ford, then call your next witness.

FORD: Thank you, Your Honor. The Crown calls Chief Inspector Jack Regan.

(Regan sworn in)

FORD: Please state your full name and occupation for the record.

REGAN: Chief Inspector John Anthony Regan, Bayview Homicide Division.

FORD: It is correct that you are the chief investigating officer in the murder of Thorvald Heintzmann?

REGAN: That's right.

FORD: Would you give us a summary of your initial involvement?

REGAN: I'm going to refer to my notes, okay?

BENOÎT: Any objection, Mr. Seeley?

SEELEY: None.

BENOÎT: Very well, proceed, Inspector Regan.

REGAN: On the evening of Saturday, 14 July of last year, I took a telephone call at 6:00 P.M. citing an emergency at 267 Thornbay Avenue. The caller identified herself as Royal Orchard.

BENOÎT: Excuse me, Inspector. That's a person?

REGAN: The housekeeper in the residence. Royal is her first name. The surname is Orchard.

BENOÎT: Carry on.

REGAN: I attended at the address at 6:10 P.M., where I found the body of Thorvald Heintzmann.

FORD: Was the victim dead when —

SEELEY: Objection. Victim.

FORD: Your Honor, it's clear that Thorvald Heintzmann died by violent means. To refer to him therefore as a victim is certainly not out of order.

BENOÎT: Gentlemen. I acknowledge that there may well be some uncertainties in this case, but the fact that the deceased was slain by a hand other than his own is not in doubt. I don't think there's anything wrong with "victim" Mr. Seeley. Overruled.

FORD: Was Thorvald Heintzmann dead when you arrived?

REGAN: I could not find a pulse and he was not breathing.

FORD: Before you describe the scene I have here photographs of the scene, which I would like to enter as exhibits. My friend here has copies.

BENOÎT: Any problem, Mr. Seeley?

(Seeley shakes his head)

BENOÎT: For the record, Mr. Seeley.

SEELEY: No objection.

BENOÎT: Very well, the clerk will enter a series of nine — *ten* — photographs. These will be Exhibits B-1 through B-10. Carry on.

FORD: Inspector Regan, as the members of the jury examine

the photographs, perhaps you could tell us where the body was when you came in?

REGAN: The body was in a study. This is at the end of a straight entrance hallway leading from the front door. The study is the last room on the right. The body was inside the room, approximately in the middle, lying face down in a north-south aspect, with the feet toward the door at the north. The body was about ten feet from the door and ten feet from the opposite wall, and lying almost against a desk on the west wall.

FORD: So the victim was shot by someone standing in the doorway to the room or just inside?

REGAN: It would be hard to conclude otherwise.

FORD: Chief Inspector, from your considerable experience in investigations of this nature, and given that you have already heard Dr. Quinn testify that Thorvald Heintzmann died one to three minutes after being shot, is it your opinion that he died where he fell?

REGAN: No, not quite. As you can see on the photographs, there is a patch of blood on the floor to the victim's left. Level with his torso. It's my conclusion that he fell onto his back first, but then rolled over.

FORD: You mean in the agony of violent death?

REGAN: I don't think so. It's pretty clear he had a purpose in mind.

FORD: A purpose?

REGAN: I believe the victim was trying to write a message. He had a pen in his hand, as the photograph shows — one of those big felt marker pens — and a piece of stationery was under the hand. There was more stationery of exactly the same type on top of the desk. It was disorderly, as though a hand or something had pulled across the pile.

FORD: So you feel that Mr. Heintzmann rolled over and tried to pull down a piece of paper and a pen from the desk so he could write a message.

REGAN: Yes.

FORD: But he died before he could write anything?

REGAN: Not quite. The letter K was written on the sheet on the floor.

FORD: The letter K? That's the same letter that starts the name of Kirk.

SEELEY: Objection.

BENOÎT: Mr. Ford, you know better than that.

FORD: Apologize, Your Honor.

(Sheet of paper and pen entered as exhibits C and D)

FORD: Inspector Regan, I have a certificate here. Excuse me, Your Honor, I neglected to mention this exhibit.

BENOÎT: Thank you. The clerk will enter Exhibit E, Firearm Registration Certificate.

FORD: Would you please tell the court, Inspector, what name appears on this certificate?

REGAN: Devon Kirk.

FORD: And what is the weapon registered?

REGAN: A Remington .25 caliber five-shot revolver.

FORD: I have two more exhibits at this point, Your Honor.

(Exhibits F and G entered)

FORD: Would you describe Exhibit F to the jury, Inspector?

REGAN: It's a book of matches. The front cover says Olde Thornhill Bar, written in three lines. On the back is a telephone number. Inside, the name of the bar is repeated on the upper flap. There are two matches removed under the Ls. On the striking band there is —

FORD: That's fine, Inspector. Where did you find this book of matches?

REGAN: On the desk near the stationery.

FORD: And would you tell the jury what Exhibit G is, Inspector, and where you found it?

REGAN: It's a gold ring. What appears to be a man's wedding ring. It was on Mr. Heintzmann's desk, under the stationery.

FORD: Would you read the name inscribed on the inside of the ring?

REGAN: Devon Kirk.

FORD: Thank you. No more questions.

BENOÎT: Mr. Seeley?

SEELEY: Inspector Regan, what was revealed in the fingerprint analysis of this ring?

REGAN: It wouldn't have been possible to get prints off the ring. It's got an etched surface and —

SEELEY: Then what of the book of matches and the stationery?

REGAN: Only the victim's prints on the stationery. On the matches, his again and another print. From a Mr. Mellish.

BENOÎT: Just a minute.

FORD: If I may, Your Honor, Mr. Mellish is our next witness.

BENOÎT: Very well.

SEELEY: And in the room? Fingerprints?

REGAN: Again, Thorvald Heintzmann's, and those of Royal Orchard.

SEELEY: No other prints of any kind?

REGAN: No.

SEELEY: By the way. The ring. The stationery was piled on top of it?

REGAN: No, not quite. When the stationery was disordered — sort of pulled over — those pulled-over sheets covered up the ring.

SEELEY: I see. Inspector Regan, I have here a report.

FORD: Objection. Is counsel entering new evidence?

SEELEY: Your Honor, I intend to submit this as an exhibit.

BENOÎT: A bit unusual, Mr. Seeley, to enter exhibits in cross-examination.

SEELEY: My friend here established the issue of the murder weapon. This is a related matter, and the police officer is the ideal corroborating witness. Unless you'll permit me to call him as my witness, too?

BENOÎT: You know that's not possible. Okay. Go ahead. But it had better be relevant.

(Exhibit H entered)

SEELEY: Would you describe this report for the court, Inspector?

REGAN: It's a police department Form 517B. Theft under $500.

SEELEY: Go on.

REGAN: It reports the theft of a Remington .25 caliber handgun from the home of Devon Kirk.

SEELEY: And what is the date of that report?

REGAN: April 9 of last year.

SEELEY: I see. April 9. Now, Inspector Regan, was there anything else in the room we have been talking about, or on Mr. Heintzmann's person?

REGAN: Just the ordinary things. His wallet, a pack of cigarettes, some change. That kind of thing.

SEELEY: So the only really unusual things are the ring and the so-called attempted message.

FORD: Objection. Counsel is leading.

BENOÎT: Sustained.

SEELEY: With regard to Exhibit C, the... uh... message, what letter follows the letter K?

REGAN: Why... no letter. There's just a K.

SEELEY: A capital K or a small K?

REGAN: You can't really tell.

SEELEY: I see. You can't tell. Your Honor, I have no other questions at this time, but I reserve the right to recall this witness for further cross.

BENOÎT: Mr. Ford?

FORD: No objection,.

BENOÎT: I think perhaps we should adjourn for lunch at this point.

FORD: Your Honor, my next witness should be brief. He's employed and has to work this afternoon. With the court's indulgence...

BENOÎT: All right.

FORD: Crown calls Mr. Muggs Mellish.

BENOÎT: Muggs?

FORD: That's what I have, Your Honor.
  (Mellish is sworn)

BENOÎT: Just a minute, Mr. Mellish. Is Muggs a correct first name?

MELLISH: It's how I'm known, sir. My given name is Montmorency.

BENOÎT: I think I understand. Carry on, Mr. Ford.

FORD: Mr. Mellish, you are a bartender at the Olde Thornhill Bar?

MELLISH: Yeah. Yes.

FORD: And were you at work on Saturday, July 14, last year?

MELLISH: I worked the noon to 8:00 P.M.

FORD: Did you see the accused, Devon Kirk, on that day?

MELLISH: Yeah, he's a regular. Was in about two o'clock that day. Stayed maybe an hour.

FORD: That's all, thank you.

BENOÎT: Will you be brief, Mr. Seeley?

SEELEY: Just two questions, Your Honor. Mr. Mellish, how is it you remember Mr. Kirk being in the bar that day?

MELLISH: Well, like I said, he's a regular. And he had his base-ball uniform on that day. Kinda stood out.

SEELEY: Did Mr. Heintzmann ever visit the bar?

MELLISH: Yeah, he was a regular, too. But if he was in that day I never seen him.

SEELEY: Thank you.
  (Noon recess)

BENOÎT: Mr. Ford.

FORD: I have one more witness. Ms. Royal Orchard.
  (Orchard sworn)

FORD: You are the housekeeper for the Heintzmann family?

ORCHARD: Yes.

FORD: Prior to the mur — the death of Thorvald Heintzmann, how long had you been employed there?

ORCHARD: Three months.

FORD: Your statement says you discovered the body. Tell us how.

ORCHARD: Saturday's my day off every second week. Other week's Thursday. I was off, but I came back to get a jacket and my smokes. Me and Vern — that's my boyfriend — we were going to go to the drive-in.

FORD: What time was this?

ORCHARD: Just before six.

FORD: Who else was in the house at this time?

ORCHARD: Nobody as far as I know.

FORD: And when you discovered the body of Mr. Heintzmann, you called the police?

ORCHARD: Yeah.

FORD: From the phone in the study?

ORCHARD: I never went in there. I ran to the kitchen and phoned.

FORD: Where was your boyfriend all this time?

ORCHARD: He was waiting in the car.

FORD: Thank you. Your witness.

SEELEY: Did you come in the front door that Saturday, Ms. Orchard?

ORCHARD: Yes. I… I don't normally, but I thought there was no one home, see, and so… Anyway, I didn't think it would matter.

SEELEY: Do you live in the residence?

ORCHARD: No, actually, I live in the annex, sort of next door.

SEELEY: Sort of next door. I see. Well, what were you doing in the main house then?

ORCHARD: My jacket. I was pretty sure it was in the kitchen.

SEELEY: The kitchen is near the study?

ORCHARD: Not really.

SEELEY: Then why did you go that way?

90

Regina Versus Kirk

ORCHARD: Well, there's two ways to get there from the front. I just went that way, that's all.

SEELEY: Um-hmm. That is all. Oh. Was the front door locked?

ORCHARD: Yes. It's always locked.

SEELEY: You have a key?

ORCHARD: Yes.

SEELEY: Is the back door always locked?

ORCHARD: Not usually.

SEELEY: Was it on that day?

ORCHARD: I don't know. I doubt it — everybody came in that way.

SEELEY: Ms. Orchard, are you right- or left-handed?

ORCHARD: It's funny. I'm both, sort of. One of those am-am-

SEELEY: Ambidextrous?

ORCHARD: Yeah. That's it.

SEELEY: No more questions.

FORD: That's the last Crown witness, Your Honor.

BENOÎT: Mr. Seeley, you indicate only one witness on your pretrial advisory?

SEELEY: Yes, Your Honor. The accused, Mr. Devon Kirk. (Accused sworn and identified)

SEELEY: Mr. Kirk, how long had you known Thorvald Heintzmann?

KIRK: Over twenty years.

SEELEY: Know him well?

KIRK: I was the best man at his second wedding — also a witness at the subsequent divorce. We played softball every Saturday in the summer. Fishing trip once a year. Belonged to the same gun club. Yes, I knew him well.

SEELEY: Tell us about the gun club.

KIRK: We both are... *were* members of the York Targets. It's a club for competitive target shooting. Handguns. Thorry and I both qualified at marksman level two years ago.

SEELEY: And did you play softball together on July 14 last year?

91

KIRK: Yes. Our game was at noon. Thorry played first base. I pitched, same as always. A lot of people saw that.

SEELEY: How is it that your wedding ring was in Mr. Heintzmann's study that afternoon?

KIRK: The umpire wouldn't let me pitch with my wedding ring on. This was kind of a delicate game. Bit of a grudge match. So Thorry kept it for me. I'd left my equipment bag in my car. I guess I forgot to ask for it back and he forgot to give it to me.

SEELEY: Mr. Kirk. Did you shoot Thorvald Heintzmann?

KIRK: Absolutely not. He was my best friend. I had no reason to.

SEELEY: Thank you, that's all. My friend likely has questions.

FORD: Yes, I do. Mr. Kirk, where were you at 5:00 P.M. on the afternoon of 14 July last year?

KIRK: I was at home asleep.

FORD: And is there anyone who can corroborate that?

KIRK: No... no.

FORD: Mr. Kirk, you smoke, don't you?

KIRK: Yes, I do.

> Bill,
>   Machine broke down here. You're missing the rest of Ford's cross- and both your summations to the jury.
> G.

Although there are a number of incriminating details that John Ford will no doubt emphasize in his summation, Bill Seeley should be able to raise reasonable doubt over a number of issues. Which did you notice?

19

Danger at the Border

WHEN FRANK MOUNT CRAWLED OUT from underneath the van with a grim look on his face and shook his head, Gene Fewster was tempted to make a crack about repairing "magic wagons" with incantations instead of spare parts. He didn't, though. Wisecracks weren't his style, even when things were going well. And right now they were going very badly. Besides, his wife, Ann, for whose benefit he'd have said it, was totally preoccupied at the moment. She was down the road a bit with Connie Mount. They were watching their portly companion, Juan Tomas, emerge from the jungle growth into which the road disappeared.

"*Norte*," Gene Fewster heard him say, jerking a hitchhiker style thumb toward the roadway on his right.

"*Norte, norte*," Juan Tomas said twice more.

That clearly upset Bluebeard. He was a recently acquired traveling companion and Ann had chosen his name. No one had any illusions whatever about there being humor in it. None was intended; the man wasn't any more amusing than their predicament. Bluebeard was Bluebeard because of the eyepatch that crowned an unbelievably repulsive scar across his hairy left cheek. The ridge on the scar spoke plainly that this wound had known neither stitches nor surgical clamps, perhaps not even disinfectant. The process of healing had not been easy.

Yet the scar was completely upstaged by something that gave the name "Bluebeard" a discomforting credibility. It was his machete. Huge, like a cutlass, it was bigger than anything they'd seen in Honduras or here in Guatemala. He carried it not in his belt or in a sheath, but in his right hand, with the flat of the wicked blade resting in the crook of his arm. Like Bluebeard's sword.

No sooner had Juan Tomas spoken than Bluebeard unleashed a string of angry Spanish that no one understood except, of course, the intended receiver. The chubby Juan was entirely unintimidated; his toothy, good-natured smile never changed. But then, it never had since he'd joined them. Ann was convinced he had once been an extra in a B movie. Connie was sure he even slept with the smile on his face. Frank had actually tip-toed around the campfire last night to look.

"*Norte*," Juan Tomas said once more, and waved Frank and Gene toward him with one hand, Connie and Ann with the other.

"*Señores. Señoras.*" Juan Tomas was going to hold a conference. Bluebeard did not appear to be invited. The little group gathered around Juan. B-movie type or not, Gene thought, the little guy was sure likable. And he didn't carry a machete, either!

"*Señores,*" Juan Tomas began, and then as though he suddenly remembered he was addressing *norteamericanos* with their strange notions, he quickly added, "*Señoras.*"

"*Norte...* safe. Good, eh? Up..." He pointed back up the road from which he'd come. "Up de road. I see... *gafas.*" He put his fists to his eyes and swung his head left, then right.

"*¡Sí!*" Juan Tomas's grin got wider. "*¡Sí, binoculares!*"

He turned right around and in his hitchhiker thumb style

pointed to a spot up the road where the valley walls began to get very high.

"*I see de son… De son go on…*"

Again Ann was the first to understand. "Reflection! He saw the sun reflect off the lenses of the binoculars!"

The others were right with her.

"Soldiers?" Gene asked.

For the first time, Juan Tomas's grin slipped ever so little.

"*¿Soldados?*" He shrugged. "*¿Bandidos?*" The grin dissipated even further. "Much gonnes, *señores. Gonnes.*"

Gene's breakfast lurched in his stomach. They had gotten so close — so close to the border and safety! Now this.

Two months ago, the Fewsters and the Mounts had begun a once-in-a-decade vacation. That they were in Guatemala was a compromise that for the most part had turned out to be a splendid success. Frank and Gene were avid Enduro bikers and they had wanted to traverse Panama, Atlantic to Pacific, on their off-road machines. Connie and Ann were equally avid about birding. They wanted to join a guided birding tour of Costa Rica. The compromise was an off-roading/birding/camping circuit of Honduras and Guatemala in a Toyota Land Cruiser. What had begun with grave misgivings on everyone's part turned out to be the most original, the most exciting, the most rewarding vacation any of them could possibly have imagined. Until three days ago.

On the outskirts of Antigua, on their way back to Guatemala City for the plane home, they were stopped by soldiers of the Guerilla Army of the Poor. In flawless English the leader told them there was fighting in Guatemala City and that the airport was closed. With perfect politeness he told them that to go anywhere near the city would be far too dangerous. He also took the Land Cruiser.

In Antigua they managed to rent a battered Chrysler Magic Wagon. Their plan — which they did not share with the renters — was to travel north on highway 1 to San Marcos, then across the Mexican border to Tapachula, a city large enough to have flights to Mexico City.

The plan had worked smoothly. In fact, the only unusual thing that happened was acquiring Juan Tomas on the next day. He appeared in a little village just as they were paying for gasoline at what passed for the local service station. After remonstrating with the dealer in very loud Spanish, he held out his hand to receive from that worthy a generous number of *quetzals*, which he promptly handed to Frank. It was obvious that he had saved them from being cheated. During the subsequent attempt at thanks and conversation, accomplished through an amalgam of Spanish, broken English, much pointing and hand-waving, Juan Tomas heard Ann say "San Marcos." At that point, the smile began, and he simply got into the back seat of the van. Both Juan and the smile had been there ever since.

Whether or not he made the Mounts and the Fewsters uncomfortable was soon irrelevant, for it was an hour or two later that soldiers appeared again. The first group was a truck convoy that barreled by them going south down the highway. They paid the van no attention at all.

Shortly after, they were stopped by four soldiers at a roadblock. There was no question that something was heating up. However, Juan Tomas seemed to charm this group, bestowing his smile and a string of Spanish on each in turn, and before long they were under way again.

"No... no... no..." Juan couldn't find the word he wanted so he smiled and said, "I feex."

And he had guaranteed his seat in the van.

Yet at the next roadblock, even Juan's charm had no power. There were only two soldiers at this stop, but there was no question that this time there was trouble. One of them was drunk; the other — in everyone's opinion, he might as well have been. They were ordered out of the van, and Juan was told, in language that made them all wince even without translation, to shut up. He did. And the smile disappeared, too. But then, as though there were some providence in charge, an officer suddenly appeared in a pickup truck and motioned the two into the back. Just as quickly and without a word, the three tore off down the road. The vacationers were safe again for the time being, but the incident scared them off the highway. They were beginning to feel more like refugees than tourists.

They went on, but by dusk they were utterly lost. They had taken so many turns and reversed so often, and had followed so many little dirt trails, that they no longer had any idea where they were. Only a vague trust in Juan Tomas kept their spirits up, for his smile came back to stay, and every time they took a turn more or less north he would shake his head and say,

"¡Sí, San Marcos!"

It was when they turned off the road to make camp that things really began to fall apart. Beginning with the van. Frank was driving and he didn't see the hole. However, they all heard and felt the result. A broken axle.

Connie was first to pick up the next concern. For some time the group had seen that to continue their press northward they were going to have to drive through a valley ahead. Now Connie saw in the gathering darkness that just inside the head of the valley the road forked.

"San Marcos?" she said to Juan, pointing first to one road, then the other.

"Sí, San Marcos," he replied, pointing to the left fork. And then he repeated "San Marcos" while pointing to the other!

"You mean they *both* go to San Marcos?" Frank asked him.

Whether Juan Tomas understood, or even whether he answered, was lost in Ann's scream. Bluebeard appeared. Silently and entirely without warning right behind her! It was a scream of fright, and Bluebeard must have realized this for he held up his left hand in the universal "okay... okay" gesture and backed up a few steps. He tried to smile, but the scar made him grotesque. No one could remember later whether Juan Tomas had spoken.

After Bluebeard made eating motions, saying "*Por favor*" a couple of times, the anxiety level dropped a bit, although the meal was eaten in the darkness and in complete and uneasy silence. When it became apparent that Bluebeard had no intention of leaving, the uneasiness turned to outright discomfort. Frank offered the consideration that Bluebeard was probably a good guy who just looked bad, but there were no seconders. They spent the night sleeping in shifts.

At the first appearance of the morning sun, Bluebeard was front and center for breakfast, which again did nothing for comfort or conversation, especially since Juan Tomas had left. He'd stuffed a tortilla in his mouth and said, "I… ah… look, eh? San Marcos. I look." Then he disappeared up the right fork.

It was just under a half-hour later that he re-emerged with his advice to take the other road — the left fork: advice that had so stirred up Bluebeard.

Gene stared briefly at the two men, Bluebeard glaring and Juan Tomas smiling, then looked at the fork. "I think," he said almost absently to Frank, "we'd better opt for beast over beauty. I'm for taking the right fork."

Frank tried to peer through the jungle at first one road, then the other. "I agree," he said finally.

Do you agree? Is there any reason for Frank and Connie and Ann and Gene to disregard and act counter to Juan Tomas's advice?

20

The Case of the Strange Hieroglyphs

DESPITE THE FACT SHE'D LIVED more than half her life in North America, Deirdre Breton steadfastly refused to use Canadian or American idiom when the opportunity arose for the British style. Especially if the British choice was just a bit arcane. That's why she told Robin Karmo to shine his "electric torch" to the "off" side. It confused Karmo for a few seconds, and that gave her just a touch of satisfaction. Karmo might be a brilliant archaeologist, but he was also an obnoxious know-it-all, and Deirdre, along with everyone else on the dig, was tacitly committed to chipping away at his ebullient self-confidence.

"The *off* side," she repeated, then deliberately allowed just a touch of weariness to shade her voice — somewhat like an impatient tutor. "Your *right* side. The hand that's holding it."

"I know." Karmo didn't miss a beat. "The switch is stuck. Who requisitioned these *flashlights*, anyway? It sure wasn't me!"

Deirdre bit off her response. Karmo was clearly a no-win case. Instead she focused her light beam on the hieroglyph, or what appeared to be a hieroglyph — the symbol over the archway that had started this little exchange in the first place. It was the third unusual marking they'd seen since entering the newly discovered maze of tunnels early this morning. All three of them over archways.

They both peered at it in deep concentration, their progressively unsubtle rivalry temporarily set aside in its mystery. Karmo's light now overlapped Deirdre's so that they could see the stonemason's work very clearly.

"Except for those opposing directionals at the bottom," Karmo said, as much to himself as to Deirdre, "there's no resemblance at all to the first two."

"Mmm... not in concept, anyway," Deirdre replied. "But I'll wager it's the work of the same tradesman. That's his mark on the bottom, I'm sure. The opposing arrows."

Deirdre turned off her flashlight. Her electric torch. So did Karmo. The only light now came from the miner's hats they were wearing.

"But you have to agree..." she went on. Her tone was no longer combative. The argument, for the present, anyway, was over; now there was simply dialogue between two scholars with a mutual interest. "You agree, surely, that these are direction signs. Code. They're clues to the route we should take — whatever's at the end."

Karmo made a face. Agreement under any circumstances never came easily for him. "Well, I doubt they have religious significance," he said, "although I'm surprised we haven't encountered anything with a burial or afterlife sense by now. But, then, probably these tunnels — this part, anyway — were all robbed clean centuries ago."

Deirdre waited patiently for him to finish speculating, and trained her helmet light onto the floor. "The first one," she said, getting back to her point, "the one we thought might be a crude type of crown..." She bent over and in the dust traced the symbol in the patch of light.

"Definitely not Phoenician," Karmo said with authority.

He was more expert than Deirdre on the Phoenicians, and she thought he brought them up far more often than necessary, but she ignored the implicit offer of further explanation and returned doggedly to her argument. "This... uh... hieroglyph was over the first archway we came to. The first point where the tunnel divided into two."

The light from Karmo's hat bobbed up and down just a bit. Agreement.

"And we took the one to the right," she continued. "Your idea."

The bobbing was more vigorous this time.

She went on. "Now, the passage from that point was straight except for two very definite turns, the first ninety degrees, the second about half that. First left, then acute right. And definite turns. Nothing gradual."

Karmo took up the retracing. "Yes, then we came to the second archway, where it divided in two again."

This time Deirdre's hat beam was bobbing. Karmo didn't seem to notice. "And that arch," he said, "had this one." He drew another figure on the floor beside the one Deirdre had traced.

"And… well… I've got to say this one does look more European than the others." He paused. "In any case we took the tunnel to the right again." He shone his flashlight up to the arch in front of them. "This time —" he stopped completely for emphasis "— this time, I think we should fork to the left. And here's why."

Deirdre was glad the darkness prevented Karmo from seeing her expression. She disagreed entirely, and her body language would only have made him intransigent. She kept silence to let him have his say; there had been too many arguments on this dig already.

Excavation had begun formally only ten days ago, after three years of difficult preparation. They were based just outside Acre in modern-day Israel. (Deirdre kept calling it St-Jean-d'Acre, its name under the occupation by the Crusaders.) The digging was on a "tell," or very large mound, where preliminary investigations had practically guaranteed activity of historical significance, possibly Phoenician, from the seventh or sixth century B.C.E.(Karmo's inclination) or twelfth- and-thirteenth-century activity under the Crusaders (Deirdre's prediction). Maybe even both!

Neither Deirdre Breton nor Robin Karmo disputed the history of the place. Acre had once been known as Ptolemais, a city of Phoenicia, but since then had been occupied by Arabs, by the Seljuk Turks, twice by the Crusaders, by the famous Saladin, and by many more — including Napoleon — until it became part of Israel in 1948.

The tension between the two archaeologists had almost become an open split when a member of the work crew, a graduate student from Cambridge, fell through a hole one afternoon into what turned out to be the entrance to a maze of tunnels that burrowed deep down under the tell. All digging had stopped then until the maze could be explored and mapped by the dig's two leaders. That was assuming they could get along well enough to accomplish the task. Deirdre Breton was simply not prepared to back down in the face of Karmo's monumental ego, especially now that the stakes, potentially, were huge. Although everyone took great care to avoid making the comparison out loud, there wasn't a single worker on the site who was unaware that the Dead Sea Scrolls had been discovered not all that far away, after a similar fall.

Thus, for the past three hours, Deirdre and Robin Karmo had been carefully working their way through the tunnels. Karmo had already published a paper, prior to the dig, in which he made a strong case for the site as Phoenician, and he was naturally inclined to interpret everything they saw in that light. Deirdre inclined toward the Crusaders, not just to counter Karmo, but because she felt the evidence pointed that way. However, nothing they had yet found in the tunnels supported either position — except possibly the three hieroglyphs. If they were indeed hieroglyphs.

"You remember," Karmo was saying, "when we took the right tunnel at the second arch, that tunnel, too, turned twice, the first time ninety degrees, the second time forty-five, but this time *opposite* in direction to the section after the first arch. Now this is why I think we should take the *left* tunnel this time."

Deirdre couldn't be quiet any longer. *"Don't you see it!"* She was surprised at her own vehemence. "We *must* go right again! It's the only logical path to take! In fact, I'll even show you what we're going to see over the *next* arch!"

"Just a minute." Karmo was completely taken aback by her force. He was not used to yielding control. "What makes —"

"No, no. *You* wait a minute." Deirdre was wound up now. "I'll tell you what. If I'm in error, you can be listed first on the paper we publish after this. If I'm right…" She let that hang in the air for a bit before adding, "By the way, I'm going to prove to you that this is a piece of Crusader work, too. Frederick II would be my guess!"

You would have to be a medieval history buff or a trivia nut to appreciate why Deirdre Breton believes the tunnels — and the symbols — to be from the time of Frederick II. But you don't need any historical knowledge to follow her logic. What symbol does she expect to see over the next arch they encounter, assuming that Karmo will agree to turn right?

21

The Fuchsia Track Suit
Kidnapping

IT OCCURRED TO GEOFF DILLEY as he slowed the car to a stop that the girl acting as flagman — flag*person*, he corrected himself — didn't really need the big STOP sign she was holding. Most drivers, the male ones, anyway, would have slowed way down at the very least, just to stare. She wasn't just pretty, Geoff thought; she was, well, *outstanding!*

And it wasn't just that. It was the getup. Her construction hard hat along with the incongruous steel-toed boots were the only parts of her attire that even hinted at fulfilling their job description. Whatever the purpose of the rest of her clothes — the denim shorts and the tank top — it certainly wasn't for protection from sun, wind and rain!

Geoff waited until she walked closer before opening the driver's side window. Pretty sight or not, she was out in the heat, and he had no intention of giving up the luxury of air conditioning. Not today, anyway.

He flashed his badge. "This going to be long? I've got a call just ahead."

Her answer was drowned in the roar of a huge earth mover as it accelerated into and out of the ditch to get around them. The torrent of dust covered the girl and made Geoff crank the window shut quickly.

When he opened it again, she peered at the badge closely, then said, "I'll get you through. Otherwise you'll be here awhile. We're crossing equipment right now."

"Can I drive on that up there?" Geoff asked, nodding at the road ahead.

The girl bent even closer. Geoff began to think it might not be so bad to be trapped here, after all.

"It's torn up right through to the intersection, but you can drive it. Just take it easy. If you go right now, I'll hold up the next mover. You should be okay."

Geoff nodded in thanks and rolled up the window again just ahead of another blast of dust. The wind took this one and carried it ahead of him down the road and high into the air.

"Must make people around here real happy," he said out loud as he started the car forward.

The "people around here" were residents of a rural estate subdivision, big homes on big lots spread out to ensure privacy. It was called Deer Trail Estates and it was where Geoff was heading in response to a call. A possible kidnapping, although the duty sergeant had classified it only Code One, so Geoff was in no great hurry.

Within minutes he reached White Tail Boulevard, the main road into the subdivision. As he slowed to turn, his own dust cloud caught up to swarm over the car. Even with the windows tightly closed there was now a film on the dash and along the steering column. He regretted going through the car wash that morning.

Number 3 White Tail was the very first house and the address where the call had originated about half an hour ago. Although the caller had implied a kidnap, he'd not actually used the word. Geoff's sergeant was not treating it urgently for that reason.

106

"Sounds more to me like a domestic," the sergeant had said to Geoff, "but there's no question we've got to respond. Guy said his wife saw their daughter get into a car on that hill up behind the Estates. That was early this morning, but he didn't call till now. You figure it. Kid's sixteen apparently, so that could mean anything. Too late for roadblocks, anyway, so no need to rush."

The house had double front doors and a portico with impossibly large pillars, one of those designs, Geoff thought, that couldn't make up its mind whether to be Greek or Spanish. When the doors opened in response to his knock, he could see the same ambiguity continued into the interior.

"Officer Dilley." Geoff flashed his badge. "Mr. Potish? Vincent Potish?"

The man was dressed in a three-piece suit, the tie tight to the neck. There was nothing unusual in that for a Thursday at noon, but it did seem rather stiffly formal to Geoff — unless maybe this was not Potish.

It was.

"Yes. Thank you for coming. This way, please. To the study. My wife's there."

Vincent Potish led Geoff down a short hallway and into a booklined room where in front of the single, large window sat a lady in her midforties. She was wearing a pink track suit that was either brand-new or else entirely unaccustomed to perspiration.

"Dear, this is Officer Dilley. My wife, Stasia."

Stasia Potish held out a carefully manicured hand. She did not get up.

"Thank you for coming, Officer. This is so... so *upsetting!*"

For just an instant, a fleeting instant, Stasia Potish's elegant composure collapsed. Had Geoff not been vaguely aware of a kind of unease about the place, he might not have noticed.

"Our daughter, you see. She went jogging up there this morning." Mrs. Potish waved a perfect hand vaguely at the window. Geoff glanced up at the heavily wooded hill that loomed over

Deer Trail Estates. This was one of the few houses in the subdivision, he saw, where the end of the lot butted directly onto the base of the hill. That had to mean money, he knew. There was a premium for that view. Close to the main road, though. In the few seconds of silence he was sure he heard the machines he'd met only shortly before.

"She got into a car," Mrs. Potish continued. "Well, not a car; it was a jeep. A *sports vehicle*."

The last phrase came out with such vehemence — and for no apparent reason — that Geoff was entirely taken aback.

"It was blue and white. Well, blue and *cream*. Navy blue and cream. These distinctions are important, aren't they? It was a Nissan Pathfinder."

Geoff was surprised — and impressed — by the amount of detail. But he didn't show it. He stepped closer to the window and peered out.

"I'm sorry." Stasia Potish was still talking. "I should have offered you a seat. It's just that everything is so filthy with dust. That terrible road work. They've been out there every day now for over a week. We can't sit anywhere without dusting first."

Geoff looked around. The place *was* dusty. Dust on the mantel over the fireplace, and dust on the ceramic tile in front of it. He could even see his footprints. There was an even, almost neat layer on the lamp beside Mrs. Potish; another covered the windowsill; the bookshelves were particularly dirty. Geoff could see where someone had wiped the back of Stasia Potish's chair and missed the corner.

"I'd rather stand, anyway," he said. "Perhaps…" He was trying to be tactful. "Perhaps you can go through the sequence of events from the beginning for me, please."

Mrs. Potish took a deep breath.

"Start with the argument, dear." It was the voice of Vincent Potish. He had retreated to the doorway after introducing Geoff and stayed there, hovering at the edge of the room.

"Yes, the argument." Mrs. Potish sighed. "Teenagers. They're so difficult. Do you have children, Officer?" She didn't wait for Geoff to respond. "Serena is sixteen. We had a disagreement this morning. Over... well, it was trivial. Aren't these things always trivial, Officer?"

As she spoke the last sentence it occurred to Geoff she had yet to use his name, but that point was obscured by the look she gave her husband. It was clear now that Vincent Potish was not a bystander in this situation.

"Serena left the house in a huff," Stasia Potish continued. "She was going jogging, anyway, so I didn't think too much of it. Typical teenage behavior. She was gone almost an hour. And that's when I saw her get into the car — the jeep. Up there."

She turned to look up at the hill. "That's another thing. She never jogs up there."

Geoff looked out the window at the hill. "You're positive it was your daughter? It's quite a distance from here up to the road there."

"She has a pink track suit like mine. Fuchsia, actually. And blond hair. Besides —"

"These, Officer Dilley," Vincent Potish interrupted. He was holding a large pair of binoculars. "My wife is the J.J. Audubon of Deer Trail Estates."

Any doubt of the tension between the couple was dispelled entirely now, for he had made no attempt to disguise the sarcasm.

"I sit here, Officer." Mrs. Potish said wearily. "In front of the window. This is where I watch the birds. It's my hobby. Early morning is the best time, you know. There's a rumor that a European finch has been seen... uh... I've never recorded one you see..." Her voice drifted into silence.

"And you had the glasses — the binoculars — when you saw your daughter get into the... uh... Nissan Pathfinder?"

"There's no question it was she," Mrs. Potish replied. "I watched the whole thing from here — through the glasses, yes."

"I see," Geoff said, and then lapsed into silence. He spoke again after a minute. "Excuse me," he said. "I'm going to talk to my sergeant. Perhaps we should organize more personnel for a search."

He moved quickly to the door, then paused." Ah… I'm sorry. This sounds so… so chauvinistic… but… you're sure it was a Nissan Pathfinder? My experience is that… uh… women tend not to pay much attention to details like that."

"Vincent has dealerships, Officer. We live and breathe cars here."

Sarcasm again. No veiling it, either. Geoff could tell there was discomfort in this house. Or else he was being set up.

An instant later, he offered just that observation to the duty sergeant on his car radio.

"They sure don't like each other," he said. "Or else they're darn good actors. That's a possibility," he pointed out to the sergeant. "Because their story breaks down."

What does Geoff Dilley mean by "their story breaks down"?

22

An Almost Perfect
Spot

FROM THE AIR, THE TOWN looked like a child's drawing. The streets were a grid pattern: cookie-cutter perfect little squares outlined with a ruler. The buildings looked stamped out: everything the same size. No industrial monsters or warehouses or other outsized structures to offend the eye. Any differences in proportion seemed accidental more than deliberate, the kind of thing that results when uncertain juvenile muscles draw freehand.

But more than anything else, what made the aerial view unique was that in every direction, the town just stopped. On each side, the edge of town really was the edge of town! There were no strip shopping malls, no crowded little bunches of commercial ugliness to blunt the juxtaposition of urban and rural. Not even gas stations! On all four sides the town of Azure simply came to an abrupt halt at the last line of the grid.

On the ground, the symmetry continued. Azure looked like a Disney feature from the 1940s. Not quite *Cinderella*; just a bit too much regal fantasy in that one. And not *Snow White*. It was *too* bucolic. More like what *Hansel and Gretel* would have been if the wicked witch had undergone therapy in her adolescence and learned macramé. That was what Azure was all about. Boutiques. Craft madness.

And that was why the town looked so — well — *perfect*! Azure existed solely to feed tourists' insatiable desire to buy anything unusual, any kind of thing they would never, ever buy within an hour's drive of their own homes, the only stipulation being that it had to come from one of those little places that no one ever went into. Except on vacation.

That's why in Azure, stores like The Almost Sober Judge ("innovative bar accessories") and Contrary Mary ("not just silver bells!") stood pastel shoulder to enamel shutter with Wind in the Wisteria and Things Being Various and The Watched Pot. No ordinary enterprise dared raise its mercantile head in this town. No hardware stores. And definitely no auto parts. The supermarket — Azure's *only* supermarket — bore the humiliation of membership in a national chain, but since it was stuck away at the end of a street, and separated from Not Your Average Bookstore by a parking lot (demarcated in grids with potted junipers) its affiliation with A & P could only be seen if one peered directly through an artful whorl of tubelighting that said "FreshorFreezer."

Only one supermarket, but two drugstores, on the quite reasonable premise that tourists, either before or after a day of boutiquing, would need remedial help more than sustenance. Neither deigned to call itself a drugstore or even an "apothecary shop." Rather, in the very center of town stood The Pharmacopoeia, while at the outer edge of both community and cutesie-poo stood Nostrum.

Azure was — well, again — *perfect*! That it was also unreal was beside the point. Perhaps that *was* the point. In any case, the town served two purposes exceptionally well: one, of course, was tourism. It had become the kind of tourist stop that was now a reference point: (*"And what did you think of Azure?"*) The other was a natural outgrowth: espionage.

Experts estimated that Azure at the height of the tourist season held more spies than Vienna in 1948. Tourism made this possible. Because practically everyone in Azure came from somewhere else, usually very far away, the polyglot that flowed from places like Interjacence ("limited edition jigsaw puzzles") across the street to Tintinnabulation ("original design wind chimes") was so thoroughly international that any face, any costume, any style was, frankly, unremarkable. A sari drew no more or less attention than a John Deere hat.

Still, the popularity of Azure with "operatives" had its own drawback: they sometimes recognized each other! Already this morning Cecile King was certain she had seen MaryClare McInerney of CSIS. That the two of them were more or less on the same side — Cecile was CIA — didn't reduce her discomfort any. If there was one familiar person, she knew there could well be others.

Cecile was sitting at La Bonne Bouche, a delicatessen ideally situated for her purpose on this warm June morning. She had a very tiny package for Dorothy Elliott, and expected one in return. The little deli was almost enveloped in its own shutters, and hidden by a carefully pruned sycamore, surrounded to near shoulder height by the mandatory iron fence. Next door, The Pharmacopoeia was just slightly set back, so that from her table Cecile had a surveyor's sweep of Appleton Street as well as the intersection with Nairn. That in turn gave her a vantage point from which to watch the tour buses make their "dumps" before pulling away to park discreetly out of sight.

The only problem was that she couldn't sit too long without risk. For one thing, the impossibly uncomfortable little chairs were designed to keep customers moving. And why not? People didn't come to Azure to sit. For another, what if it really was MaryClare McInerney she'd seen? Who else might be around today?

Cecile leaned over an inky espresso so her eyes could make a quick unobtrusive scan of the street. So far so good. Nothing suspicious for the moment. At first, she'd thought the business at the bus dump a few minutes ago was a setup. Normally, two buses unloaded simultaneously at this special spot, but when she'd first sat down, the lead space had been occupied by Eternal Spring Tours, a load of seniors who took so long to disembark that the line of waiting buses was stacked south on Nairn farther than she could see.

By the time Cecile had finished her cruller, however, Eternal Spring was able to pull out and the dumping speeded up. During the first few sips of espresso, she'd watched a matched pair of Silverliners discharge their happy loads. She'd half expected Dorothy Elliott to be on one of these buses, but everyone who got off wore either a jacket or a T-shirt that said Cobbleton Pin Busters over a triangular logo of bowling balls. No way Dorothy was part of that! In their business you didn't want to stand out.

As she began a second espresso — Cecile knew it had to be the last — another set of buses pulled up. Still no sign of Dorothy Elliott. Cecile knew now she was going to have to —

There she was!

They'd worked together only once before: a quick exchange in a poorly lit café back on the east coast, but she knew it was Dorothy.

Cecile watched her thread down the street, working her way around the Eternal Spring seniors, who were managing to knot up the pedestrian traffic pretty badly. For a second she lost her, then picked her up again. Dorothy was a pace or two behind one of the Cobbleton Pin Busters, a big man with a rather slouching gait. Cecile watched as the two of them strode past The Espadrille, around the little crowd in front of Diaphany, where the resident glassblower was presenting a demonstration of his art, then directly across the street into La Bonne Bouche.

Even before Dorothy turned abruptly right at the doorway

and up the sidewalk, Cecile had left for the washrooms in the rear and the fire exit.

Cecile King and Dorothy Elliott caught a warning at about the same time. What made them simultaneously decide against the exchange at La Bonne Bouche?

23

An Interrupted Patrol

GARY ELLESMERE HAD TWO EXCUSES for being on the road on a hot August morning. The first was simply to get "field time." A reasonable enough explanation — on the surface, at least. After all, one of the first policy changes Gary had made when he became chief was to decree that everyone — and he meant *everyone* — who carried a badge would spend a certain amount of time in the field. So in effect he was simply following his own orders. "Leadership by example": it was a phrase he used often with the staff sergeants.

Gary's other excuse was to road-test — just one more time — the patrol car borrowed from the Tottenham City force. Another reasonable enough excuse, for his second move as the new chief was to convince the county treasury department that the force needed six new custom-built sedans to replace the highway patrol fleet. It was a coup on Gary's part. Tottenham City already had these new machines and he knew his people drooled every time one of the powerful vehicles was anywhere near.

Two sound and sensible excuses, then. And Gary Ellesmere knew his staff didn't believe either one of them. The plain truth was the Chief had a smashing hangover!

His fiftieth birthday the night before had been an occasion of such fanfare and hoopla that Gary allowed himself, in his words, "to be overserved." That was the real reason he was on the road this morning. He had forsaken an air-conditioned office for a very warm car, but the relative isolation had made it a fair trade. No telephones, no irate citizens, none of what he liked to call the "dilemmas of leadership." And even for a fifty-year-old this machine wasn't such a bad item to be spinning around in.

The sun made Gary squint as he turned off the highway onto a side road. Just about five minutes down the road was the purest and coldest drinking water in the whole county. It came from a spring that fed from underneath a long-abandoned, one-room schoolhouse and ran out a rusty pipe with enough force to make a permanent drinking fountain. Not even the exceptionally hot dry weather they were having this summer could slow it down. Local farmers called it the Tap. The little stream to which it gave birth they called the Creek. Either source would serve Gary right now. His dry throat was pushing upward to join a pounding headache.

It was when he pulled out of a careless wander across the yellow line that Gary saw the figure out on the road. In fact, his eyes took in the scene for a full second before his brain told him to brace up. Something was wrong!

The figure was a boy — no, a man. Short, though. He was running hard toward the patrol car.

In the few seconds it took to close the gap, Gary could see it was indeed a man. His policeman's mind went automatically through a checklist: adult male, white, maybe mid-thirties, about five-six, 165 or so, big muscles, mustache, brown and brown, balding on the peaks, denim shorts — cutoffs. Someone had lopped the legs off a pair of jeans. Green basketball jersey with 60 on it. No team name. Sneakers really worn and dirty.

The man was puffing very hard.

"Back — ba — oh, God! Back there!" He pointed vaguely behind him and leaned heavily on the driver's side door. "My wife. Back there. In the kitchen. She's dead! I know it! She's dead!"

Gary shrank back a little in spite of himself. The pungent smell of the man's sweat overlay the morning heat. He didn't like the guy leaning on the door, either. It hemmed him in.

"Back off. Lemme out." Gary spoke with calmness but authority. He didn't even notice that his headache was gone.

The man moved to lean over the fender. Runs of sweat rolled down his arms and whorled over the thin film of road dust. His breathing began to slow as Gary got out.

"No. No. Get back in! We gotta go…" The man waved at a spot farther down the road. He was obviously weak from the run and what appeared to Gary to be the onset of hysteria.

"My wife! She's dead! Blood all over. She's not breathing, she's — God! — *chopped up!*"

Gary could see the man was about to lose control.

"Okay, get in."

The man ran around the front of the car and got into the passenger seat. From the edge of his concentration Gary couldn't quite push away the impression that his passenger was going to stink up Tottenham City's new patrol car, and it was due to be returned that afternoon!

Maybe it was being ordered into the car, or the sense that someone was now taking charge, but something seemed to calm the man a bit.

"Down there." He pointed with more specific emphasis this time as Gary pulled back on to the road. "Just past the creek. Red brick house. How did — I mean, how come — I mean, a *cop*! I didn't expect a cop! I was running for help. My wife's dead. I'm sure of it. See, I was checking fence. Right there. That field. See?"

Gary could see a large pasture that had obviously not been grazed for some time.

"I couldn't a' been gone more than half an hour. Checking fence, I mean. Only one wire down and the field's not that big to go all the way round. I went back to th' house for a drink of water and there she was on the floor by the sink — turn there, the gate's open — and the phone's out! I ran out to the road. Nobody! I was running up to the Purdleys' for their phone. That's when I saw you."

The front right tire settled in a pothole as Gary stopped by the house. The man bolted out immediately and ran to a screen door that didn't seem to be quite closed.

"Hold it!" Gary shouted. "We go in together!" In one motion he stepped out the driver's side door and pulled his communicator out of its cradle.

The response at the other end was immediate. "Go ahead, Chief."

For a moment Gary paused to wonder just how the dispatcher knew who it was, but then he realized that the fancy new patrol car had a transmit code.

"I've got a possible homicide here." He could almost hear the attention double. "I'm three klicks east of Number 10 on County 22. Red brick farmhouse. Name Haspen, H-A-S-P-E-N, on the mailbox. I want an ambulance and a backup right away. For the present I'm calling this a domestic, but if you don't hear from me again in three minutes — mark, that's *three* — treat this as an 'officer down.' I'm going in now. Acknowledge."

The "ten-four" was instant. Gary dropped the communicator and flipped the switch on the light bar so that arriving vehicles could key in on the location more easily. As he ran up to the screen door he could see that on the wall just above some trampled flowers, the telephone line had been neatly severed.

"Okay. Stay just ahead of me," he said, and motioned to the man to go through the doorway.

Gary is being prudently cautious, but it's apparent he doesn't expect a trap. Why is he "calling this a domestic"? What makes him suspicious of the man he's supposedly helping?

24

The View from the Second-floor Promenade

AT THE INTERSECTION OF THE north and west walls of the Greater Wellington Shopping Center, the railing that surrounded the promenade on the second floor traced its way around an extension that jutted out over the main floor mall just enough to accommodate a pair of areca palms on either side of an incredibly uncomfortable plastic bench. At the grand opening ten years ago, some copywriter, in a burst of excess typical of the species, had labeled this spot "The Promontory." The name, however unmerited by the tiny space, had stuck.

"The Promontory" was D.U. ("Herbie") Michael's preferred observation post. From it, he could see the front entrances to sixty-two of the mall's ninety-three stores. He'd counted them several times. Herbie liked numbers. Equally important — perhaps more important — he could look right down on "The Green." Another pretentious label, this time identifying the mall's focal point and main meeting area.

The name was supposed to imply *village* green. Its principal attraction was the "Dancing Waters Fountain," in which arcing jets of water leaped from one little pool to another in random order. When it worked, the Dancing Waters Fountain was a delight. Unfortunately, its ambitions in the direction of terpsichorean splendour were regularly marred by breakdowns caused partly by lousy design, but mostly by one of the banes of Herbie's working life: teenagers who came down to The Green to hang out.

These kids who met at the mall to cruise and, from time to time, boost whatever goods they could from unwary merchants, were one of the main reasons Herbie appeared regularly on The Promontory with walkie-talkie in hand, ready to call in his patrols from all points in the mall when they were needed to thin out the crowd below. Herbie hated doing it. His people were supposed to spend most of their time on the alert to prevent shoplifting. D.U. ("Herbie") Michael was head of security for Wellington Center. He considered himself a professional, and found the traffic-and-rowdyism role offensive.

"What you see right now —" he was talking to a very attentive young man beside him, but at no point did he cease to sweep the mall with his gaze "— is typical Wednesday morning traffic."

He made a rainbow sweep with his right hand. "You'd think the whole city had nothing to do so it comes here."

The young man agreed. "It's hard to believe this many people go shopping on a Wednesday at 11:00 A.M."

"They don't." Herbie said grimly. "That's why we're here. Oh, most of them are shoppers, all right, and some of them are sitters. Like the old guys down at the fountain." He pointed at three old men sitting immobile on benches just as formidable as the one in The Promontory. They were staring straight ahead, apparently at nothing.

"I feel sorry for them, actually," Herbie continued. "I'm sure they'd rather be sitting in some sunny piazza or be out playing *bocce* somewhere, but they have nowhere to go, so they come here and sit and stare. When they're awake."

His young companion edged closer to the railing and raised himself on tiptoe to look at the old men. Indeed, one of them was sound asleep.

"Now, those two —" Herbie's tone changed "— are more the type you have to keep your eye on." He pointed at two teenage boys. Both wore baseball hats — backward — and large padded running shoes with the laces untied.

"They should be in school... those poor teachers. Yet at least kids like that are obvious. Most of the time they're just a pain. Noisy. Not too often you have to do anything about them until the numbers get big. Herd instinct takes over then. Still, they don't boost all that much except maybe in the record stores. Cassettes. And cigarettes. Watch them in the smoke shops."

Herbie's protégé nodded. For him it was orientation day. He was willing to take in all he heard.

"Where you get trouble is with the weirdos and the professional lifters. Now they... ah... see that guy down there, the one with the green windbreaker? I've been noticing him for about five minutes now. Strange."

The object of Herbie's attention had just walked up to the entrance door of Lambton Florists and was standing almost against it. He stood there for about ten seconds, seeming to stare straight at the door, then put his hand on it — tentatively — for a few seconds, and pushed. No result. Finally he pulled. The door opened and he went into the store.

"That's the third time he's done that," Herbie said. "First over there at Computer Age, then at Kinetic Sports and now Lambton's."

"Maybe he's doing research on doors?" the young man offered with a chuckle.

"Could be." Herbie smiled. "Could be a nutcase, too. Either way, he's one you've got to watch. There, too! There's another. That really fat guy. I've never seen him before. That counts. Somebody that big you'd remember so this one's a stranger."

Herbie was focusing on a very large man in the promenade

below, walking slowly, looking at each of the stores, but not going in.

"You'll soon learn." Herbie put his hands together. "There's a way that fat people walk, so you know they're real. Sometimes that large tummy is full of boosted goods. Would you believe last year we caught a guy with a *microwave oven* where his stomach was supposed to be! And his partner... she had a whole set of microwave dishes! Just like they were going into business. They..."

Herbie paused, his attention drawn to the front of Neve's Smoke and Variety on the other side of The Green. The young trainee's attention had gone there even before his. Neve's Smoke and Variety was clerked until 3:00 P.M. each day by a young lady whose name was Daisy, and whose two most notable characteristics were an ever-present wad of gum so big it completely precluded intelligible speech, and skirts so short they didn't come even close to earning their keep. Every morning at eleven, when Daisy came out and bent over to pile out the afternoon edition of the *Daily Telegram*, she drew a crowd. Starting with the old guys at the Dancing Waters Fountain. They were smiling now, completely awake and enjoying the morning.

The *Telegram's* headline shouted up to the Promontory: LONGTIME LIFER ESCAPES! The radio and TV news that morning had been full of an escape the previous night from the penitentiary at the outskirts of the city. The *Telegram's* lusty, tabloid competitor had doubled its normal headline size and screamed KILLER LOOSE! No subtlety there. On the other hand, the city's third daily, the sober and somewhat arch *Empire* aimed its headline at the disconcerting certainty of an economic slowdown.

As Daisy retreated to the Neve's counter, to the universal disappointment of the denizens of The Green, Herbie continued his instruction. "Pregnant women. Watch for them. It's such an old trick you don't see it much anymore, but never shut your eyes to it. A woman who's genuinely pregnant is going to sit down and rest once in a while. Most of the time they seem pretty uncomfortable, too. And — now there's something — those two guys in suits. When you see that you have to ask yourself what's normal. Two guys in suits in a shopping mall on a Wednesday morning? If they're here to do business they'll show it by the way they act. With purpose. If they're hustling — then it's different. It's all behavior. Just watch behavior. Sooner or later the boosters give themselves away."

The young trainee watched the two men carefully. They appeared to be lingering — waiting for something. His attention was diverted briefly by the two teenagers in baseball caps. They had suddenly emerged from Jazzy Records and one of them appeared to be walking abnormally fast. He raised his hand to point, but Herbie nodded. He'd seen them, too. Meanwhile the man in the green jacket had come out of Lambton Florists carrying a small, neatly wrapped bouquet — it looked like the $4.98 carnation special — and walked over to Dave Seglins Photography, where he repeated his strange behavior at the door there. The fat man, too, had now come back up the mall, and was standing by the Dancing Waters Fountain, arms akimbo, staring intently into Computer Age.

"For heaven's sake!" Herbie shook himself. "Behavior! I must be slipping! You stay here," he said to his protégé. "Keep an eye on everything and everyone out there. I'm going to call the police."

What has led D.U. ("Herbie") Michael to believe he has reason to call the police?

25

Death in the
Bide-a-Wee Motel

TO DETECTIVE FIRST CLASS DOLORES Dexel, the dead man on
the floor in front of her was hardly an example of what a big
drug operator was supposed to look like. There was no flash to
him, no evidence of heavy money, nothing that said "big time."
On the contrary, everything about him ranged from mild all
the way to even milder.

Starting with the brown slacks. Nothing approaching Italian
silk here; these were strictly off the rack. So was the tweed jacket, the kind made to last ten years before leather patches are called upon to adorn the elbows. Dolores couldn't see the shirt or
the tie, but she knew what they'd be like. From where she stood,
though, she could see the man's sturdy Oxfords had recently
been resoled. The heels were new, too; she could read CAT'S PAW
semicircled in the center of each. Even the man's wedding ring
said "reliable, ordinary, *solid* citizen." His fingers were curled
around the edge of an open Bible — the ultimate touch, Dolores

thought — and the ring reflected light from a cheap lamp beside the bed. It was a gold ring, not too wide, not too narrow, no adornment or stones or etched design. Just plain. Solid.

What was most emphatically unordinary, however, was the way he had died. No murder was ever run-of-the-mill, but this one was a step into the unusual. It was an execution. There was a small-caliber bullet wound in the back of the head at close range. Another in the middle of the back and one more at the base of the spine. Insurance shots, Dolores knew. Certainty that the victim was dispatched. The killing shot had been to the front, close range into the heart. At least that's what Dolores thought because of all the blood. She wasn't about to turn him over until the forensic guys got here. She needed photos, too.

That reminded her. What was taking the photographer so long? And the light bar she'd called for? The light especially. The seedy little motel room had a single bedside lamp to supplement the wan glow that tried to reach the floor from the overhead fixture. She needed to be able to see better.

"Forensic just called. They're on their way."

Dolores looked up to see her partner, Paul Provoto, in the doorway. The rattle of the Coke machine just down the hallway was so loud she hadn't heard him approach.

"The lights'll come with the photographer," Paul continued. "And I've got a blue sitting with the night clerk that called in. You can probably talk to her again now. She's not so cranked anymore."

He took a step into the room, then thought better of it. "Gawd. Did this guy bleed or what!"

Paul was right. It was one of the first things Dolores had noted. The blood was not spattered all over as she'd seen so often before (too often — only six months in homicide and already she wanted out). Rather, the blood had flowed — poured! It had run around the outline of the body on the beige tile floor all the way down to the sensible shoes, and in the other direction, along both outstretched arms. It was in the victim's hair (short, getting quite thin. And brown! Dolores had noticed that on the way in). The trail of blood had even curled around the open Bible, as though it were seeking its own path, unhurried, uninterrupted, framing the book neatly so that the double column of text looked even denser from top to bottom. Only the victim's hand, lying on the opposite page, was free of the red substance that was still oozing from the body.

Dolores looked up at Paul. "I'm going to go talk to the clerk," she said. She had to get out of the room. It was suffocating her. "We'll talk in the lobby. Call me if the photographer comes in the back way."

She walked carefully around the body, out past her partner and down the hallway to where the night clerk was waiting. Through the grimy skylight she could see streaks of gray. Be morning soon, she thought. Another night with no sleep.

The night clerk hadn't slept, either, certainly not since she'd called in over an hour ago. For most of the time Dolores and Paul had been at the Bide-a-Wee Motel, the young woman had been drifting back and forth over the border of hysteria.

She was on the calmer side when Dolores entered the lobby, but not comfortably so. She sat scraping away at a gouge in the surface of an end table with an incredibly long, and patently false, thumbnail.

The officer sitting in the only other chair got up. Two chairs, the badly scarred end table, some outdated magazines and another cheap table lamp made up the "front desk." There was no counter, only a window, a thick Plexiglas one that slid back and forth to enable the duty clerk to accept cash in advance. Nobody used plastic at the Bide-a-Wee Motel.

Dolores sat down gingerly. She didn't want to push the clerk. The chair didn't appear to be up to any serious test, either.

"Miss —" For a second she'd forgotten. "Ah... Miss Duvet,"

she began. "Can you tell me again where you were when you heard the shots?"

The question nearly turned out to be a bad mistake. The night clerk flushed and tears started falling along an already well-worn channel in her makeup.

"I *didn't* hear a shot! I *told* you that! I went for a Coke and I *saw* him... the bod..." The tears began to flow faster.

"Yes, yes. That's right. I'm sorry." Dolores put her hand on the young clerk's arm. "Of course you did. My fault."

The soothing tone had effect, and Miss Duvet's tears retreated to snuffles. Dolores also retreated from her ploy to see if the woman's rendering of events had changed since their first encounter.

"Let's go through it one more time." She was going to try a softer tack. "You went down the hall for a Coke. Then what?"

Miss Duvet took a deep breath. It seemed as though she was going to hang together now.

"Then I saw him. The door was — like — open. Like, I mean, who'd leave their door open in a dump like this? And the light's on, too. So I, like, look in. And jeez! There he is!"

"Did you go in?" Dolores took a chance with that.

"*No way!* I mean — jeez! Would *you?* Like — the guy's *dead!* I mean, I *think* he's dead. Like, there's so much blood he's *got* to be dead, right? 'Sides. Even if he's not — like, this ain't Mercy Hospital, right? What do I know from first aid? So I run back here and call 911. I mean — like — so you're me. What would would *you* do?"

"What time was that?" Dolores asked.

"*I don't know!*" Miss Duvet's fuse was shortening. "I didn't keep track! This ain't a hockey game! They don't even have a crummy clock in here, anyways!"

Dolores noted that Miss Duvet did not wear a watch, either.

"Did you..." she decided to go on. "Did you go back to the room then?"

"*Are you nuts?* No way I'm goin' back there! Like, already I gotta full-time picture here. I mean watch this!"

She lifted her face and closed both eyes with emphasis. In the poor light Dolores hadn't noticed till now that Miss Duvet's eyelashes were almost as long as her nails.

"Like, I gotta pair of three-by-fives here. Full-color glossy. You wanna picture? I got it, like every time I close my eyes!"

"It must have been terrible for you." Dolores had decided that the sympathetic approach was definitely going to get better results.

"Terrible. Like — try *mind-blowin'!* I mean, like, this guy. Mr. Straight. Mr. *Brown Clothes!* What's a straight guy like that doin' here, anyways? Like he's even got the Gid out!"

"The 'Gid'?" Dolores thought she knew, but she wanted to be sure.

"Yeah, the Gid. The Gideon. Like — yuh know — the Bible. He's holding it on one side: 'Gospel according to Matthew.' Like have I gotta picture or *what?* Yuh work in a fleabag like this yuh learn to read upside down. I mean — it's like fun to watch them make up addresses for the reg card. Anyways, I seen the Gid — the Bible. He's got it open. Matthew, right? And the guy's gettin' bald. I seen that, too. I mean I gotta picture. What else yuh wanna know?"

Dolores fumbled in her shoulder bag, ostensibly for a tissue but actually making sure her tape recorder was still running. She was about to ask when Miss Duvet had come on duty, but Paul came in.

"Kodak's here." He pointed out the front door. "And the lighting guys are just pulling in."

Dolores stood. "Tell the photographer to wait," she said. "I want some special shots from the doorway. Also from the feet up." She paused. "And Paul... come on out here a minute."

Paul led the way out the door to the parking lot.

Dolores had her notebook out. "I want you to call in some backup teams. Now! As many as the captain will give us for a neighborhood search. And post the blues around the circumference. It's probably too late, but I don't want *anyone* leaving here. Unless Miss Glamorous in there is lying through her teeth, somebody was in that room between the time *she* saw the body and *we* did."

Why does Dolores Dexel think that?

26

Bailing Out the Navy
— for a Price

Shifted to one side in the sagging easy chair, an ankle resting on the opposite knee, and slouched way down in the sinking comfort the old chair invited, Bob Ashby conveyed a sense of easygoing acceptance. It was a posture that said, "Okay, take your time. I'm here to listen."

He was dressed casually, too: cords, a knitted sweater. The only hint that he might not be just another employee of Ashburn Engineering, on a break here in the office, was the polish on his loafers. That and the fine leather document case on his lap.

In the flotsam of esoteric, machined parts that filled every conceivable cranny of the office of Ashburn Engineering, so many in fact that at first glance they almost hid the collage of outdated girlie calendars, these two items stood out. The leather of the document case particularly, for its elegant finish picked up the wan glow from a single naked light bulb in the ceiling, where it played forlorn host to a crusty coat of fly specks.

It took courage for Bob Ashby to sit with such apparent ease in the old chair. As with the rest of the office, "clean" was not an adjective the mind would admit in describing it. Nevertheless, Bob was not at all uncomfortable as he sat there, chin cupped in his hand, conveying a sense of complete, professional neutrality. A major point in his favor was that the chair faced the window behind Thurm Elliott, and Bob knew that any light from the setting sun that managed to struggle through the scum on the panes would reflect off his glasses and conceal his eyes. They were the only characters in his role-playing that he couldn't control. And since he flat distrusted Thurman Elliott, Jr. (with good reason), he knew his eyes would say so. Clearly.

For another thing, Bob Ashby had been in so-called offices like this many times before. As an independent consultant in industrial design, with a specialty in deep-sea salvage, he'd encountered operations like this one almost daily for more years than he wanted to think about. Although in regard to this particular visit, Thurm Elliott's reputation as a crook was an exception in the industry, rather than the rule.

"They're all in threes, the pieces —"(*cough, cough, harrumph!*) "— every wuh — every wuh —" (*cough, cough, hack, ah-hack!*) "— jus' a minute." Thurm Elliott stood up to hawk and spit into a cardboard box in the corner. He missed and the phlegm stuck to the side of the box.

For a second Bob's facade came unhinged as his gaze was irresistibly drawn to the gob of yellow dangling incongruously over the 4 in the stencil that said "Pineapple Juice 48 oz." This was the third time Elliott had stood up to spit into the box. The first two times he'd succeeded.

"Every one of them —" he seemed in control now, "— three links. So that means —" (*cough*) "— we're gonna hafta..." Another fit of coughing began. This one started as a rapid series of *huh-huh-huhs* and grew through a series of *harrumphs* into a veritable blizzard of belly coughs so hard Bob found himself trying to breathe on Elliott's behalf.

"Cold." He said, turning over a blackened palm in explanation. As though Bob Ashby really needed to be told. "Can't get rid of it." Thurman Elliott took a rag out of the back pocket of his coveralls and blew wet and vigorously, then wrenched his nose as though he were shutting off a balky faucet.

Bob's posture of casual ease was on very thin ice now. He had dealt many times in his business with people who had become brutalized over years of working with rusty, dirty, recalcitrant machinery in impossible conditions. Thurman Elliott, however, was one of the worst. Not just in manners, in ethics, too. The man had been forced out of business four times that Bob knew of, twice by bankruptcy, once running from a civil suit and the last time by government investigators. Still, he was the only one on the Pacific coast that anyone knew of who was capable of doing the job Bob had come to approve.

The steam-driven catapults on the *Whitby*, the navy's oldest aircraft carrier, had been sabotaged. How, or by whom, no one knew, but that wasn't Bob's concern, anyway. The binding chains had been cut into pieces — no simple task. That was another element of mystery in the case — who *could* have cut them? — for each link was forged of an alloy of steel, platinum and titanium. They were incredibly hard, and certainly impervious to the attack of ordinary tools. Yet the chains lay in pieces. Twenty pieces. And until they were restored to four separate chains of equal length, the catapults were useless and so, for all intents and purposes, was the *Whitby*. She could sail, and she could land planes. But she couldn't launch them.

That's why this particular job was so crucial and, for political reasons, so urgent. On the deck of the *Whitby* sat her full complement of aircraft. The press had not yet learned of it, and likely wouldn't unless the carrier had to sail down the coast, through the Panama Canal and up the Atlantic coast in turn, to either Norfolk, Virginia, or Halifax, Nova Scotia, where the repairs could be effected. A lot of navy reputation, therefore, hung on the skills of Thurman Elliott, Jr. and Ashburn Engineering.

That aside, past experiences with him had made the base com-
mander turn to Bob Ashby just to be sure. Getting stung could
be just as embarrassing as having to sail around to the Atlantic.

"Piece work —" (*cough, cough*) "— 's only way to bid this
stuff. Yuh gotta open a link 'n' then close it 'round 'nother —"
(*har, har, HAR!*) "— 's only way —" (*HAR!*).

Bob braced himself for another hawk and turned away from
the pineapple juice box. It didn't come. Instead, he watched in
disbelief as Elliott, with a single hand in practiced motion,
snapped the filter off a cigarette as he put it in his mouth, and
began to lift the papers on his desk in search of a match.

"'S' if they need four equal lengths, I make it sixteen cuts 'n'
welds. Ten thousand per. 'At's one-sixty total. 'Suming I have
no trouble. Now that's not outa line. 'Sides, they got nobody
else. Ah, there!"

Thurm Elliott reached under a precariously balanced box of
envelopes for a small metal container, opened it and took out a
wooden match. He looked for a bare spot on the surface of his
desk, gave up and then out of long habit stood halfway and
scraped the match alive on the seat of his coveralls.

Bob Ashby took off his glasses. He was finished listening
now. He let himself stare at the unshaven face on the other side
of the desk. Interestingly, it was Elliott now who, behind the
cloud of cigarette smoke, had adopted a neutral stance.

What irritated Bob, as a taxpayer and as a professional, was
not the fee rate, although he'd come in with an upper limit of
$7,000 or $8,000 in mind. It was the patent make-work fraud-
ulence. Only $40,000. A pittance in military budget terms. A
mote. A speck. But it was still a case of someone taking unfair
advantage.

"Ten per is high, Thurm." Bob spoke for the first time since
he'd sat in the easy chair. "But I guess I can get the navy to go
along with *one-twenty* total. No advance, though. Not at ten
thousand per."

The hard glint in Thurman Elliott's eyes lasted only for a few seconds before it washed away in another fit of coughing. This time when Elliott stood to face the pineapple juice box, Bob turned his head. Easygoing acceptance time was over. Elliott had got the message, so if Bob wanted to turn away to keep his stomach under control, there was no reason not to now.

It is clear that Bob Ashby has a different view of how the chains should be repaired, and his idea will apparently take less work than Thurman's Elliott's proposal. Elliott's way will cost $160,000; Bob Ashby's will be only $120,000. What is the difference in their strategies?

27

The Case of the Missing .38 Smith and Wesson

GARY WESTLAKE MADE A MENTAL note to find out who had been the last to use Number 9119. The car had literally come to life when he turned on the ignition, and he hated that. One by one he turned off the radio, the windshield wipers, the fan, the rear defrost, while he waited for the engine to warm. Whoever it was, he noted with even more annoyance, had even left the glove compartment door hanging open. All this, along with an accumulation of junk on the passenger seat: gum wrappers, a ratty toque (certainly not a regulation item but sometimes the highway patrol used them), a flashlight that should have been returned to its holder under the dash and what appeared to be a forgotten, half-completed accident report.

With one hand, Gary scooped up the mess and tossed it into the back seat. "There's one slob in this department," he said out loud, "who's going to be very sorry the Chief had to use a patrol car today!"

Gary had a fully developed passion for order and neatness. He began to plan, even enjoy, the substance of the anticipated chewout as he clamped the transmitter switch twice.

"Go ahead." Central Dispatch, at least, was doing exactly what it was supposed to do.

"Westlake here. I'm exiting the lot right now. Expect to return by 3:00 P.M. If there's…"

"Chief! We were just going to all-call you. Lowinski wants you. Says it's urgent."

Gary toyed for a moment with ignoring the request. New people on patrol had a way of failing to separate true urgency from simple impatience. Besides, he had a throbbing toothache. "Patch her through," he replied tiredly. He knew he couldn't entertain the thought of ignoring a call from a rookie.

Almost instantly the young policewoman was in contact. "Sir? Chief Westlake?" Gary hated Lowinski's habit of speaking in the interrogative. It made her sound like a teenager, which, come to think of it, he realized, she almost was! She was only twenty-one. "This is Chief Westlake." He tried not to sound gruff, but his tooth really hurt.

"Ah! Chief? The Packers case? I think I have something? You know the gun? The missing gun? A .38 Smith and Wesson, right? I'm holding a guy here. You better… uh… do you want to see for yourself?"

The Packers case was an unsolved murder, the first murder, solved or unsolved, in the seven years since Gary had become chief. One of the missing links was the murder weapon. Ballistic information had told them what it was, but that was as far as anyone on the case had been able to get.

"Slow down, Lowinski," Gary said, as much to himself as to the young woman on patrol. He could feel excitement in spite of himself, in spite of his aching tooth and the mess in 9119. "First of all, where are you?"

Lowinski was not about to slow down. "On King Road? East? I'm at… at…" The voice grew faint, then loud again. "At… in front of 414, okay? 414 King Road."

"All right. Hang on." Gary took a deep breath and thought

for a moment. A .38 Smith and Wesson was hardly something out of the ordinary. If it was only an unlicensed gun, then he'd be smarter to let Lowinski handle it herself. Good experience. But then...

"Lowinski. Are you all right? Do you need help?"

"No, sir, I'm fine. I have the susp — I mean, I have a possible arrest in the car. There's no trouble, okay? You want I should bring him in?"

"No. Yes! I mean... wait a minute, Lowinski."

Gary's toothache, which had been coming and going in waves, was gathering strength for another surge. He waited, but it didn't come.

"Uh... Lowinski? The Smith and Wesson? What's fishy about it?" Gary wondered if he, too, wasn't beginning to speak in the interrogative.

"No license."

Gary almost groaned.

"I stop him a few minutes ago, right? Tail light out. And I think I smell booze, right?"

Against his better judgment Gary answered, "Right."

"So. Routine check. I open the trunk. And there it is in the trunk. The gun?"

It occurred to Gary that Lowinski was not only interrogative in her style, she also spoke entirely in the present tense. "What makes you think it has anything to do with the Packers case?" he asked.

"Smith and Wesson, right?"

"Lowinski, we've been through that." The wave of ache had only been teasing before. Now it had arrived in force.

"Yeah, but that's it! The guy says he just found it! Like this morning?"

Were it anything but the Packers case, Gary would have made a second mental note: to have Lowinski take speech therapy. Instead he responded, "*Found* it? Where?"

"You know the construction on King Road? At the edge of

town? On the east? Toward Nobleton? Just at the bottom of the hill?"

"Lowinski, I know where it is!" One more question on top of the toothache would have tipped him over the edge.

"Well, the guy says he saw it lying in one of the big puddles there, right? Says he figures somebody ditched it. So he picks it up? Says he hasn't had time to turn it in. Okay?"

Gary heard himself say, "And you've, like, got him in your car now, right?" Whatever Lowinski's response, he didn't hear it. He was staring in shock at himself in the rearview mirror. "Lowinski, you've done well," he finally said. "Sit tight. I'll be there in two minutes."

He pulled the shift lever down into Drive, but before accelerating wiped a smudged fingerprint off the speedometer glass with a gloved hand. More dirt, he thought. "Lowinski! You still there?"

"Yes, Chief?"

"Lowinski, what car did you have yesterday?"

"Number 8228. The same one I always have. Why?"

"Never mind."

What has made Gary Westlake decide to endure toothache and discomfort to investigate Lowinski's potential arrest a little further?

28

On the Trail of the
Stolen Horses

WITH THE NAKED EYE, ESPECIALLY from a standing position, it was impossible to tell for sure whether the stolen horses had been ridden along this particular trail. There were tracks, all right, hoofprints all over, almost all of them heading northeast, or else southwest, for that was the general direction of the trail. At a few points there were hoofprints that doubled on top of one another, rimming a semicircular pattern, showing that as a rider had reined up, the horse had done a bit of prancing. Most of the tracks snaked between two alder stumps that the farmer hadn't pulled yet, but there was nothing unusual in that.

Marv Chantler knelt to get a closer look, holding the reins of the rangy bay gelding with one hand. As he did so, the horse bent to nuzzle the back of his neck. It made Marv jump. "G'wan!" It was the first word he'd spoken since leaving the settler's grimy little yard at sunset the night before. The woman in the sod shanty had assured him in her laconic, distrustful manner that the horses had gone this way.

Marv ran his fingers over some of the prints on the trail. None of them was clearly fresh. They were more than a day old at the least. But from this close he could see the difference in the various horses: the size of the hoof, the ones that were shod and those that were not, the style of the smithies. He stood up and took a couple of steps toward the alder stumps, then knelt again. The bay followed without urging.

Here there was a different set of tracks. A wolf probably, or a large dog. With his eyes, Marv followed them across the trail. This animal had been in no great hurry. The tracks were straight for a few paces; they diverted in midtrail — likely to sniff some horse dung — straightened again, then diverted once more, almost certainly to sniff a varmint hole at one of the alder stumps. It was obviously abandoned, for dusty cobwebs stretched across the opening. The tracks then straightened once more and disappeared into the alder thicket. This was a fresh set, Marv could see. Last night, no doubt.

He stood up and rubbed the small of his back. The gelding came closer, expecting to be scratched. The hoofprints Marv was looking for — he just couldn't be sure. One of the stolen horses had thrown a shoe. Right foreleg. And there was a V-shaped chip out of her hoof. That had made the trail fairly easy to follow, and Special Constable Marvin Chantler of the Battleford detachment, North-West Mounted Police, had made steady progress for the past several days because of it.

There were three stolen horses, all of them, to the monumental embarrassment of the Battleford detachment, the Mounties' own! There was the huge jug-headed roan that Sergeant Gordon liked so much, a piebald mare of indeterminate ancestry — she was missing the shoe — and a bay gelding, full brother to the one Marv was riding now.

Their trail had led due north from Battleford and Marv had not lost it until just before he rode into the squatter's little farm last night at sunset. He thought about that moment as he pulled the bay round, put his foot in the stirrup and mounted.

The horse turned again, so that Marv had to redirect him to head back to the farm.

At first, last night, Marv had thought no one was there. But there were chickens scratching in the yard, and he'd heard at least one pig snuffling behind the sod shanty. Maybe *in* it, for all he knew. It was not uncommon for these little shacks to do double duty. Then the woman had appeared at the door: thin, worn, old way before her time, wearing a dress so faded from scrubbing it was hard to tell if it had ever had a pattern. Her hands were big and red and wrinkled from labor. A toddler clung to her leg, venturing to peer out at Marv only when he was sure he wouldn't be observed.

Marv had been at scenes like this many times since he'd come to the northwest. Settlers, squatters in the middle of nowhere, fulfilling the terms of their land grant by living on their quarter section. If it could be called living: ground down to the last ounce of resistance by poverty, hardship and total, absolute, isolation.

He'd brushed the dust off his tunic to be sure the red could be seen in the fading light. The reputation of the NWMP for honesty and fairness was known even to people like these. Maybe, he had thought, the sight of the red coat would allay some of the inevitable distrust.

It didn't. The woman never left the doorway. Getting her to speak was almost impossible. Still, she had acknowledged that yes, she'd seen three horses a couple of days or more ago. No, she couldn't remember much about them. One was very big. Gray. Another was patchy-colored. Two men. They didn't come near. Her man stood down by the fence with his shotgun. When Marv asked about where they'd gone she was a little more definite, pointing to the trail on which he was now returning.

This time as he approached the shanty there was more life: smoke from a hole in the corner of the roof, more chickens, and a dog that hadn't been there last night. It was barking furiously, running at the horse and backing away, making him dance nervously.

The woman appeared in the doorway again. In the morning light the dress was even more faded than the night before. The distrustful look was just the same, though. Nor was she any more forthcoming.

"You're sure those horses went up that way?" Marv smiled, attempting to break the ice.

She only nodded. Once.

"I know what I'm looking for," Marv said, "and I really couldn't see the tracks I want."

The woman lifted her face toward the sky and shrugged ever so slightly. "Rain," she said, barely opening her mouth.

Marv was silent for a long time. Then he sighed audibly. He had to let her know he didn't believe her now, but he didn't want to scare her, either. In a way he felt sorry. Not just that she was situated out here in the middle of empty space; it was more that she made him think of his mother back in Dorset. It was a lifetime since he'd seen his mother, since he'd answered the ad calling for young men seeking adventure doing police work in the colonies. There was nothing adventurous about his present situation, however, just uneasiness. Well, at least she didn't *look* the least bit like his mother. That was something, anyway.

What has convinced Marv Chantler that the woman in the sod shanty is misleading him — deliberately or otherwise?

29

The Royal Blue Escort

"IF YOU ASK ME, THERE isn't a single blue Escort — uh, *royal blue Escort* — in the whole country, let alone Wythenshawe. I mean, how can we sit here for almost two hours and not see one up ahead there on — what's that street again — Brownlee? I mean, it's impossible! Likely the most popular car in the whole world and — Ow! *That's the third time!*"

Harvey Bottrell was slowly losing his customary good sense of humor. Whether he was right about the Ford Escorts or not, there was no mistake about the number of times he had banged his elbow on the parking meter. Sitting there in the nondescript, mud-colored Rover with Vin Murray, and with nothing to show for two hours of diligent watch, Harvey had begun to fidget. He had the feeling their stakeout was going to go sour, as so often happened. The thought disturbed him, and three times now he had bumped his elbow as he twisted round to look out the back window of the Rover.

Vin Murray, meanwhile, was concentrating on the task of relighting the bottom half of a cigarette. Earlier, he'd set a book of matches in front of him on the steering column. They'd fallen off and now he was looking for them.

To Harvey's further discomfort he simply responded, "Aye." Vin was not known for prattling.

"Well, at least —" Harvey was just the tiniest bit annoyed, "— at least can we back this thing up a bit into the proper parking space now that the car behind us is gone? So I don't have to sit nose-to-nose with this meter? I've got MANCHESTER PARKING AUTHORITY burned into my brain!"

"Aye." Vin had found the matches and lit up. His face was now completely obscured in a thick cloud of relit Player's Plain. It even moved with them, exactly in place, when Vin backed the Rover a few paces.

Harvey couldn't help himself. "Don't you think you should open your window, too?" he said.

The two men didn't know each other very well; they'd met for the first time only yesterday. Vin was a special assignment agent (antiterrorist) with Scotland Yard, working out of the Manchester office. Harvey, a Canadian, was with Interpol, working out of New York. The two were acting on a tip that the notorious Hans Keffer, of the Red Brigade, was in Wythenshawe, or possibly was coming to Wythenshawe, an eastern suburb of Manchester, for a meeting.

Keffer was famous among police forces in Europe, had been for years, because of his careful disguises and his obsession with "blending in," so he'd never be noticed. Neither Harvey nor Vin was surprised at the use of a Ford Escort. They knew it was a typical Keffer choice. The man knew England in great detail, and he'd know what car to pick. What did surprise them — and made them both dubious, though they'd not yet shared their doubts with each other — was the amount of information in the tip. Not just the car, the royal blue Escort, but the fact that the meeting was to take place on Robb Road in Wythenshawe. That was why the two were staked out here.

Vin nodded in agreement with Harvey about the window.

"Aye," he said yet again, then with careful deliberation transferred the cigarette stub to his other hand and rolled down the driver'-side window.

As the smoke swirled out, Harvey could see another No Parking sign on the pole opposite. Through the windshield — uh, wind*screen*, his inner voice reminded him — he could see the slashed red circle on every pole prohibiting parking all the way down to Brownlee Road. It intrigued him that the signs were so low.

"Y'know," he said, "in North America, the kids would be disappointed those No Parking signs aren't higher up the poles. Our kids like to make basketball jumps to see if they can touch signs like that."

Vin stared across at the signs for so long that Harvey wondered if it was possible he had never noticed this before. Vin took a final pull on the cigarette, then, with his thumb and forefinger, squeezed the glowing coal into the ashtray. Harvey waited for the "Aye."

Instead Vin said, "We play football." He put the cigarette butt into the Player's package. "It's closer to the ground."

Harvey's chuckle was swelling into a belly laugh, when it stopped in his throat. He and Vin stiffened into alertness in the same second. Coming down the street toward them was a Ford Escort. Royal blue. It wasn't new. Maybe two, three years old. Clean but not recently washed, certainly not shiny. Very Keffer. Nothing stood out.

The driver looked to be in his midforties. Everything seemed exactly right. But for one important thing. The two agents looked at each other.

This time Vin spoke first. "Nervy, that bloke. Or maybe he just doesn't know."

"I'd say he doesn't even know," Harvey replied. "But, then, maybe he saved our necks, too. We might have come down on him like a ton of bricks."

They both turned to watch as the car came abreast of them,

then passed on down the street until it topped a grade and dipped out of sight.

Harvey's shoulders drooped. "Looks like we're here for a while yet," he said, and then looked up at Vin. "That place where the other team is staked out? By the airport? What's it called again?"

Vin was looking around for the matches once more. "The Ship Inn."

"The Ship Inn," Harvey repeated. "It's a pub. Isn't it?"

Vin shook his head. "A right proper pub. Good ploughman's. Good place for a pint."

Harvey grimaced. "Some guys have all the luck."

"Aye," Vin said.

Why did Havey Bottrell and Vin Murray not stop or try to follow the royal blue Ford Escort that came toward them up Robb Road?

30

An Unlikely
Visitor — or Two

From the moment his office door swung open, Struan Ritchie knew this was not to be the kind of peaceful lunch break he always looked forward to. For one thing, Mrs. Bain, his exceptionally serious and exceedingly proper secretary, had not tapped the door first and then waited a discreet two or three seconds as was her custom. For another — Struan couldn't swear to it, for he didn't recall ever hearing it before — he was almost positive he'd heard Mrs. Bain suppress a giggle before she said, "Captain Ritchie, this gentleman has been here for the past three days to see you. All of the detectives... *hee...*" There it was again! Struan was sure of it this time. Mrs. Bain had giggled! "All the detectives feel you should handle this one."

For the moment, Struan couldn't see the gentleman Mrs. Bain was referring to, but through the open door he did get a sweeping glimpse of the squad room. Every single one of the detectives out there was watching — well, not just watching, they were staring, no, *gawking* — like a crowd at a fall fair. And they all had huge grins on their faces.

The detectives' expectations were bound up in the person of the little man who suddenly appeared from behind the ample Mrs. Bain, as though he had been hiding there.

"I'll be at my desk, Captain Ritchie." Mrs. Bain closed the door. Now Struan could hear loud guffaws out in the squad room. For a second he forgot his visitor. Only for a second.

"You're Captain Struan Ritchie, then. The medievalist, right? We're so pleased." As he spoke, the man stepped forward — minced forward, really — and sat in one of the two chairs in front of Struan's desk. He put an old-fashioned triangular-style briefcase on the other.

Struan tried not hard to stare. In spite of his years in police work he was inherently gracious. He'd never developed that suspicious weariness and confrontational pose so typical of police with long tenure on a big city force.

But his visitor invited staring. Provoked, it, in fact! The chairs in front of Struan's desk had over the past twelve years held con artists, wife-beaters, murderers, pickpockets, politicians, even — last week — a bishop. Today's guest, however, was like no other.

It wasn't just the unusual shape of the man; he had what appeared to be a normal torso on top of exceedingly short legs, so that sitting in the sturdy wooden chair, his feet — big feet — didn't quite reach the floor. Nor was it just his clothes. They were hardly a leading example of contemporary fashion, but that wasn't what distinguished them. It was more the combined effect of a vest, which did not quite match the suit, covered in turn by a cardigan that had no affinity whatever for the rest of the attire.

Still, it was not his appearance that attracted attention. It was the *manner* of the little fellow, Struan concluded. He had about him an aura of serenity, total serenity, the kind of at-peace-with-the-world that one imagines in cloistered nuns (Struan had met one or two of those) or successful graduates of prolonged therapy (Struan really wasn't sure whether he'd met any of those or not).

Whatever the source of calm in the man, he had made himself completely at home. In the brief instant when Struan was sizing him up, and trying to ignore the laughter in the squad room, the visitor opened the old briefcase and took out a book, which he set on the desk. The book appeared to be very old, written on what quite possibly was vellum. Struan got a rush at that. He really *was* a devotee of things medieval, a hobby that protected his mind and soul from the daily brutalities of urban police work, but not one that he could share with very many of his working colleagues.

The man then very calmly cleared a space on the desk. For more books Struan thought, but what appeared was a small, oval, beautifully crocheted doily followed by two Spode china luncheon plates perfectly matched. These were set out symmetrically on the doily. Now Struan really *was* staring!

"We are truly pleased you could see us." The voice was so calm, so gentle. Struan realized he hadn't been aware that the whole time the scene was being set, no one had spoken a word.

"Uh… it's… uh… not a problem. You…" Struan was stammering. He never stammered. His attention was being torn between the book, which he so desperately wanted to open, and the strange little man, who was now setting out carefully trimmed cocktail sandwiches on the Spode plates, along with — this was why Struan stammered, he was sure — tiny cocktail onions, individually wrapped!

"We hope you like tuna. These two have chopped walnuts." He nudged one plate slightly with a manicured hand. "These have celery. Surely you like tuna? Almost — *Of course he does!*"

Struan flinched at the latter outburst. It was so angry.

"Not necessarily." (Serenity again.) "Not everyone likes tuna. There are some people who — *Of course they do! Everyone does! You're doing it again!*"

This time Struan stole a glance into the briefcase. In spite of himself he was looking for the source of the second voice. He shifted slightly in his chair so he could see behind the two chairs without turning his head.

The two voices continued. "*The book! Tell him about the book!* Yes, Captain Ritchie, the book. It's quite beautiful, isn't it? A 'Book of Hours' we're told. Mid-to-late fifteenth century, the agent said. Book of hours — that's like a prayer book, isn't it? It has prayers for special occasions and times of the day, doesn't it? Such a lovely thought. The wealthier classes — *Get on with it! Real or phony? That's why we're here!*"

That one made Struan jump. By now he was totally bewildered. The little man with the two voices and the beautiful book had sat throughout this entire exchange eating his elegant tuna sandwiches (one each of the chopped walnut and the celery) without a ripple in his peaceful demeanor.

With one hand Struan stroked the surface of the book's front cover. It certainly appeared to be calfskin, worn at the covers, but like so many pieces from medieval Europe, magnificently preserved. He opened it about midway to a beautiful spread. On one page, an illustration showed floating cherubs over what appeared to be children immersed in a bath, and surrounded by women, likely servants. Opposite, in rich ornamentation, with fine leaf work and a flower form motif in pink, blue, orange and green, was a single sentence in Latin: *Munditia pietam similis esse.* The M, in the style so typical of the era, took up over half the page, swirling in and around the sentence and finally enclosing it in an embrace of gold leaf.

Ever so gently, Struan drew the back of his hand over the letters to feel the irregularities of the scribe's delicate work. He was quite prepared to lose himself in its beauty, when suddenly his reverie was intruded upon by a loud guffaw from the outer office. With some reluctance, and also, he acknowledged later, because he didn't know what else to do, he took out an interview sheet.

"Uh… I'm sorry. This is standard procedure. I… uh… have

to have a record." He found he was still stammering.

"Of course. *Hurry up!* I understand. *Get on with it!*"

Struan put on his glasses. He never used them for close up, but it was another contact with reality.

"Your surname, please?"

"Miles."

"And your first name?"

"Miles."

"No, no. Uh… your given name."

"It's Miles."

"I think, maybe…" Struan took off his glasses and straightened his tie.

"Miles Miles! Tell him! And not just that! Miles N. Miles! No middle name like everybody else — just N! Miles N. Miles. Our father didn't want a baby! We were a surprise! It's his idea of revenge! The book! WILL YOU GET TO THE BOOK!

For the first time, right in the middle of this outburst, Miles N. Miles looked directly at Struan. His expression was entirely benign, unmoved. Not a hint of annoyance. The only suggestion of anything out of the ordinary was a dollop of mayonnaise on the man's chin.

"Cleanliness is next to godliness, right?" Miles N. Miles said. "That's how the Latin on that page translates, doesn't it, Captain Ritchie? From the Bible, isn't it? The Old Testament?" The benign smile continued. *"For God's sake, I'll tell him! We'll be here forever! Look, we're rich, we're going to buy this for the museum! Now, is it real?"*

For the first time, the reason for the visit dawned on Struan. Also for the first time he felt he had a bit of control. "Ah, I see!" He was silent for a moment. He really wanted to linger over every page in the book, but at the same time he knew his busy precinct had no time for that.

"Why don't you gent — I mean… why don't you go to the university for an opinion? The medieval period is just a hobby with me, but they have experts. For instance, I can tell you that on this page here, with the sentence you're referring to, the Latin — it's not very good Latin. But, then, in a lot of monasteries the scribes themselves often didn't know Latin. A lot of the time they were just transcribers. Artists, too. Some of them. But, you see, if you went to the university…"

"*Not the university! Greedy! They're greedy! They want fees! They forget they're public servants!*"

"Wait… wait, Mr. Miles. The university — the range of expertise there is very wide, and you'll get better advice there. You see…" Struan took a deep breath; this was the part he didn't like to say. "You see, it's very unlikely that this is a book from the medieval period. It's generally agreed that medieval period ends around the year 1500, and I'm sure this book was produced well after that. Now, at the university, maybe there's someone who can tell you just when."

There was no reaction from Miles N. Miles. Just silence, which to Struan seemed quite prolonged, then a nod, as he began to return the luncheon plates to the briefcase. One of the sandwiches remained: a celery. For only the second time he looked straight at Struan. "*You don't like tuna, do you? Hah! I knew it!*"

What has led Struan to the conclusion that the book brought to him by Miles N. Miles is not likely to be a "Book of Hours" from the medieval period?

31

The Mission in
the Clearing

THEY HAD LEFT THE Land Rover in the bush and come in the
last mile or so on foot. That had been the intent in any case,
but because of the condition of the road they really had no
choice. Curiously, instead of improving as they got closer to
the little mission, the road had become worse, so that there
was no question of proceeding without headlamps on. The
moonless night was just too dark and the growth too thick.
Even on foot they'd had trouble getting through quietly, but
they'd made it without being discovered — or so they thought
— and now the four of them were kneeling in the long grass
at the edge of the clearing.

The squad was down to four, because the two Kikuyu "Home
Guard" who normally rode on the roof of the Rover had disappeared shortly after the message came in on the wireless. Just
melted away in the darkness. WO/I Ron Forrester had experienced this once before in an almost identical situation, and he
wasn't really surprised. At bottom, he didn't blame them. These
auxiliaries were called "government loyalists," but Ron knew

that if their fellow Kikuyu in the Mau Mau ever caught them, they'd suffer a lot longer and a lot harder than the white soldiers in his squad.

What truly irritated Ron, however, and frightened him, too, was the loss of the wireless. Its battery pack, actually, for that was what the operator, Lance Corporal Haight-Windsor, had dropped under the rear wheel. The squad could do without Haight-Windsor. He was back with the Rover, nursing his broken arm, still drunk in all likelihood. Ron swore that when they got back to base, Haight-Windsor was going to be busted yet again, this time to private, but only after a nice long dryout in the stockade.

A message had come in two hours ago, the product of one of those radio wave flukes that amaze everyone and surprise no one. It was a call for help originating from St. Ignatius-in-the-Forest Mission, probably from one of the still smoldering huts in front of them. It had been picked up by a ham operator a continent away in Somerset. He managed to get the local police to believe him, and then, via a series of telephone calls, the message had been relayed to Nairobi and thence to Ron's base back in Nyeri. Major Bowman himself had called from there.

His booming voice over a burst of static had jerked them all awake. Good thing, too, for the last watch of the night was Haight-Windsor's and that was when he'd gotten drunk. It was during loadup that he dropped the battery pack.

The order was simple: "Divert from the patrol and proceed with all possible haste to St. Ignatius-in-the-Forest Mission. Use extreme caution. Under attack by Mau Mau terrorists."

An improbable name, St. Ignatius-in-the-Forest, but the mission was run by an equally improbable group of Jesuits from England. Against all advice they had refused to close it when the Mau Mau uprising had begun in earnest. On the contrary, the two fathers who ran the place had only just been relieved by two young seminary graduates fresh from Liverpool. Ron had never met them; he didn't even know their names. But he'd heard they were even more adamant than their predecessors about keeping the mission open. Now it seemed they were paying a price for their determination.

From where he knelt in the long grass, the light from the slowly rising sun told Ron that whatever had happened here, it was over, and the Mau Mau attackers were gone. Along with everyone else, it seemed. Or maybe they'd gotten out like the two Kikuyu auxiliaries. All but one of the buildings, the tiny schoolhouse, had been burned, destroyed. There was no sign of life anywhere, not even bodies. If there was anyone here, he (or she — Ron couldn't remember whether the nuns had finally left or not) would have to be in the schoolhouse.

Several yards to his left, PFC Willie Throckton shifted slightly to avoid a cramp. He looked over at Ron with eyebrows raised, and swung the barrel of his Lee Enfield Mark IV toward the schoolhouse. Ron signaled back "just hold on," then crawled to his right, where the two others, Barrow and Highland, were concealed behind the mission's upturned GMC pickup. From here, Ron reconnoitered once more, using the new perspective to confirm his strategy.

Without taking his eyes off the school, he spoke to Barrow. "S.O.P. I'm putting a grenade over there for diversion. Then Throckton's going in first. We cover. He shelters on the shadow side. When he's in, you go to the other side."

Barrow just nodded. They were an experienced team and had done this before. Even Haight-Windsor, like the rest of them, had done two tours in Korea only a few years before.

Ron leaned back to be sure Highland was listening. He was.

"You're staying," he said to Highland. "I'm pretty sure the place is empty. If there's no return fire, I'm going straight in the door."

Highland simply nodded and ran his index finger along the grenades in his belt.

No more than ten seconds passed between the time Warrant Officer I Ron Forrester threw the grenade and when he burst through the door of the schoolhouse. There had been no return fire.

Ron stood in the schoolhouse for a few seconds more, then called, "Looks clear! I'm okay! Stay alert!"

It was not Mau Mau style to stick around after an attack, but he was taking no chances.

The shambles in the schoolhouse was to be expected. Quickly Ron took in the scene. Benches and tables were piled in disarray along both side walls. With their *pangas* the attackers had chopped up the school's paltry few books and scattered them around. A huge gouge had been cut out of the already dilapidated chalkboard. Particular care had been taken with the crucifix. It was barely recognizable. What really held Ron's attention, though, was the two dead priests in the center of the room.

Strangely, there was no evidence of torture, but that might have been because the squad's approach had been heard or seen, after all. Both men lay facedown in a pool of their own blood. Their arms had been cut from elbow to wrist, ritually, and it appeared they had bled to death. The right leg of one priest was bound at the ankle to the left leg of his partner with a leather thong that must also have had ritual significance, for small animal bones dangled from it at precise intervals. Both men still wore their shoes and Ron couldn't help reflecting on the improbable contrast of the mystical thong and the sturdy, sensible black Oxfords. One was scuffed from top to bottom at the back of the heel, the other — in fact both shoes belonging to the other priest — sparkled with a fresh buffing. It almost seemed as if he, like his attackers, had done some ritual preparation, for his cassock, too, was clean and new, and his hair neatly combed, unlike the priest on the left, whose appearance was unkempt, disheveled.

Both men, however, lay in the same position on the floor, and when he saw the nails, Ron suddenly knew what the attackers had had in mind. He looked again at the chopped-up crucifix and shuddered. It was well the Mau Mau had heard the squad coming.

Taking a few steps, he picked up one of the nails, then, for the first time, noticed the key ring lying under the remains of a bench near the wall. With his foot he dragged it out and picked it up. It had an ignition key. That he recognized. Another key — he had no idea what it was for. There were two brass disks. Both said D.M. Vincent, S.J., on one side. On the opposite, one said, A+, and the other said, Dipth. W.C. Typhoid 12/07/54.

He put the ring in his shirt pocket, then looked around cursorily for more things like it. When he saw nothing, he reluctantly bent over the bodies and began to pat their pockets for belongings. Nothing. A white band on the wrist of one of them said there had once been a wristwatch there, but it was gone.

Ron rocked back on his heels for a minute, wrapping his arms around his legs at the knees. That was when the fly crawled up from inside the rather dirty Roman collar to settle on the nostril of the priest nearest him, and he saw the twitch. At first he thought it was his imagination, but when it happened again he yelled for Throckton. Throckton was the squad's medic.

The young PFC burst in immediately, his rifle at the ready.

"One of them's alive. I'm sure of it!" Ron realized he was still yelling.

Quickly Throckton took a pulse behind the jaw of each priest. "This one!" he said excitedly, indicating the one whose nose the fly had found. Then more slowly he added, "But not for long. It's thready. He's lost too much blood."

"No! No!" Ron was shouting again. "I'm A-positive! You can transfuse, can't you?"

"Yes, but... yes." Throckton could sense Ron's excitement. "But that's not enough!" He shook his index finger in a kind of maternal admonition. "To get enough, we'd kill you to save him! By the look of it he needs four, five pints! I can't take more than one, maybe one and a half out of you, and that's dangerous, anyway!"

"Let me see!" Ron grabbed Throckton's identification tags. "No! You're A-negative!"

"So's Barrow," Throckton replied. "And Highland's AB something. Haight-Windsor's O-negative."

"O-negative!" Ron grabbed Throckton's arm. "That's universal donor, right? Can you get enough out of me and out of Haight-Windsor to keep the priest alive until we get to the airstrip at Rumuruti? That's an hour away in the Rover!"

Throckton pulled his arm away reluctantly. "But Colour Sergeant! It's not that simple! O-negative is okay, but… how do we know the priest's blood type matches yours? If we give him the wrong type, we'll kill him, anyway!"

"Trust me." Ron said. "Which arm? Let's get started." Then he shouted, "Barrow! Get out there and get the Rover and bring that fool wireless operator with you!"

What has made Ron Forrester confident that his A-positive blood is the same blood type as the priest who is still alive?

32

Trespassing on the
MBA Property

THERE WAS NO WAY OF getting to the site without climbing up
and then down a series of fairly steep knolls, and at the top of
the fourth in a row, Jack Atkin paused once more to catch his
breath. He leaned against a large maple, one arm extended as
casually as he dared without falling over, and willed his lungs
not to puff. Ron Minaker and Harold Bidigare were at least
one knoll behind, and he knew they would both be breathing
hard into the crisp autumn air when they caught up.

That would give Jack a bit of an edge, he knew; he wouldn't
even have to say anything. In fact, the edge would be sharper
that way, for he would hone it by initiating conversation in an
entirely normal voice, while the other two would have to gasp
for breath to respond. Jack had recovered from a serious coro-
nary two years before and was now a committed distance walker. It did wonders for his condition and he couldn't help being
just a bit born-again about fitness. Especially with Minaker and
Bidigare, who were notoriously out of shape. The three old
friends had been doing this to one another for years: one-upping

in a genial but very satisfying way.

The joshing wouldn't last long, though. This case was too serious for frivolity. Jack Atkin was a private investigator. Harold Bidigare was president of Rosseau Casualty Inc., a large insurance firm. And Ron Minaker was a senior partner in the law firm that handled all of Rousseau's litigation. They were here in what Bidigare called "absolute confounded nowhere" — Minaker called it "classic, post-Pleistocene terrain" — to look firsthand into a piece of evidence in the Dahlman case, a high-profile, potentially messy lawsuit that Bidigare's firm and its largest client, Mary Blair Associates, couldn't afford to lose.

Mary Blair Associates was a big land developer. For several years, in anticipation of urban sprawl from the city, MBA had been holding on to a big piece of hilly land that it planned to turn into an estate residential subdivision. The southwest corner of the piece, where the three men were now gathering, abutted a large tract of public land, destined one day to become a nature park.

For the present, the area had become a haven for young teenagers on ATVs, three- and four-wheeled, high-powered, all-terrain vehicles that Jack and many others privately referred to as kid-killers. MBA had posted No Trespassing signs and No Motorized Vehicles Allowed signs all along the property line, but the kids paid little attention to them, especially since this hilly part of the MBA property was dotted with mature maple and ash and a few oak trees, just sparse enough to make weaving through them at the highest possible speeds a real challenge to young ATV drivers.

Four months ago Sasha Dahlman, a fourteen-year-old and, to add to the complexity, second son of the city mayor, had piled up a Suzuki 230 and turned himself into a quadriplegic for life. Now the Dahlmans were suing MBA. Precedent in case law put MBA in a delicate spot despite the signs, for the property was not fenced. But the company did have a trump card to play: it was not clear whether the accident had occurred on the

MBA property or on the public land.

The Suzuki had been found, damaged but upright, precisely bisected by the property line, but in fourth gear and facing the public property. Searchers had found Sasha Dahlman about twenty meters inside the line on the public property side, but he swore that he'd flipped well back on the MBA side, that the machine had kept on going and that he'd crawled for some time before passing out. Both an orthopedic surgeon and a neurologist had testified that much of the spinal damage was likely due to "post-trauma aggravation," so the lad had indeed probably crawled after the crash. But from where?

This morning Ron Minaker had jolted both Jack and Harold with news he'd just received from Dahlman's lawyer. Yesterday, Sunday afternoon, Dahlman's elder brother had found Sasha's helmet in a hollow where several of the knolls lined up like a large pocky rash on the landscape. The spot was well inside the MBA property.

To Jack's immediate question, Ron replied that two other boys were with the older Dahlman and all three had already signed statements that they'd seen it clearly on MBA property from one of the hills and that they'd then brought out the local police to photograph it and take it in. Whether Sasha had been wearing the helmet or not, Ron pointed out, would be of no consequence. This was to be a jury trial, and in the hands of the very able Dahlman lawyer, Graeme Campbell, the location of the helmet would be damaging evidence, indeed.

The situation was urgent enough to bring the three men out here almost immediately, Jack in his hiking shoes, cords and a DiTrani hiking jacket, his two more sedentary buddies still wearing suits and ties, and both regretting it.

Jack pulled the zipper of his jacket up to the throat. It was chilly where he stood here on the hill. Indian summer had visited briefly and then left, about two weeks before. There was no snow yet, but winter wasn't far off. He ticked the zoom lever on his Canon Photura to get a better focus on Ron Minaker, laboring up the hill toward him. Minaker had found a pair of toe rubbers in his trunk and a red-and-black checked hunter's cap. At either end of his tailored suit, covered in turn by a rakish London Fog trenchcoat, Minaker was a caricature of himself, especially since somewhere back farther he'd undone the earflaps on the hat. By framing the look of discomfort on his face, the hat made him look like a very unhappy beagle.

Jack took two shots, one after the other. An intense, all-day wind the week before had cleared the trees of any remaining leaves, and he had a clear view. He could also see through the viewfinder that Ron wasn't puffing nearly as hard as Harold Bidigare, and Jack knew that would not go without comment.

"Tell... tell... tell the St. Bernard to pour! We're almost there!" Bidigare shouted. He really was breathing hard.

Ron Minaker was about to add something but checked himself and posed. Jack was taking a closeup. What Ron didn't realize was that one of the earflaps was now sticking out at a right angle. Jack would use that at a cocktail party sometime in the future.

"Sheesh!" Bidigare wasn't finished. "Can't you arrange a helicopter next time? Where are we, anyway? I bet there isn't a good restaurant within two hours! What time is it? I'm hungry!" Each sentence had come out in a rapid burst.

Ron Minaker looked at Jack and spoke with the deliberateness that results from very controlled breathing. "It really wasn't so bad. Frankly, I didn't realize this moraine had so many drumlin formations at this point. Back there we..."

"Is this... is this..." Harold Bidigare was fighting to slow his breath rate. "Is this dissertation going to be on your bill?" He turned to Jack. "I have heard more geology that I don't want to know in the past hour than..." He gave way to a fit of coughing.

Minaker chuckled. "I'm surprised you could hear, with the noise you make breathing!" He looked to Jack. "You don't have a resuscitator in that fancy jacket, do you? We've still got to walk back."

164

"No," Jack replied, " but I did bring Geritol, because I knew you two were coming." With his index finger he pushed up on his left breast pocket, exposing the top of a flask. "But here. First. While you've still got your eyesight…" He held out several large glossy photographs and a hand-drawn map. "You agree that's the spot down there? Where they supposedly found the helmet, I mean?"

His two companions took the material and studied it, sobered by the reminder of just how serious the situation really was.

"Not much doubt," Ron said. He looked back and forth from the photographs to the hollow below, then handed them to Harold Bidigare, who did the same.

"Good," Jack Atkin said with emphasis, and pulled out the flask. "You'd better fuel up, you two patsies. It was definitely worth coming out here, but now we've got to walk back."

The reason for coming out to this spot on the MBA property was to check the finding-of-the-helmet story and to find a flaw in it if there is one. It appears that Jack has done so. What is it?

33

When History
Becomes Math

WHAT JOHN FOGOLIN COULD NEVER reconcile, even from
the informed perspective of the tenth grade, was how Sister
Augustinetta could be so, well, so downright obnoxious and
difficult, and still be a nun! All the other nuns he'd ever known,
especially here at Quail Run Academy, were just what everybody
thought nuns should be: helpful, kind — most of the time —
and full of the peacefulness that spread to people near them.

Some of them were fun to be around. Like tiny little Sister
Mary Theresa in the first grade. She wasn't much bigger than
her students, but all she had to do was appear in the schoolyard
and in seconds she looked like a queen bee in a swarm, with all
the first graders clamoring around to hold her hand. Then there
was Sister Anthony from the sixth grade, who was deeply ad-
mired by all the senior boys for the way she ripped the last possible ounce of power out of the convent's black Chrysler sedan.
And Sister Mary Bernadette, who had a fastball that no one,
not even Barney King in the senior school, could lay wood on.

But Sister Augustinetta? The only thing John could figure

was that she was a math teacher, and math teachers, he was convinced, just were sort of that way. Quail Run still reverberated from the short tenure of Ms. Thibodeau-Elmont, who'd taught math to the sixth, seventh and eighth grades two years ago. She became known immediately as "El Tigre" and in only three months was mysteriously replaced by the dramatically less efficient but infinitely more patient Sister Veronica.

Among other things, what bugged John — he looked down at the paper in front of him — was that Sister Augustinetta turned everything he liked into math lessons! Take this project here, in North American history. It was supposed to be *history*, for heaven's sake. And he *liked* history! But this...?

The tenth grade had been divided into"investigative trios." Each trio was given its own problem to solve, and each member in a trio held a distinct piece of information needed to solve the problem. The three parts, properly put together, along with a bit of very straightforward research, would supposedly yield the solution.

John Fogolin's trio had been given this problem:

> *Which of the firstborn children of Magdalene, Catherine and Korron, if any, would have been American citizens, or British citizens, when they were born?*

All three held that question. John, in addition, was given this piece of information.

> *All three of Hezekiah Beame's daughters, Magdalene, Catherine and Korron, married at the age of twenty-two in Pawtucket. Each had her first child there, exactly two years after her wedding ceremony.*
>
> *Magdalene celebrated her eighteenth birthday during the voyage from Bristol to St. John. At the time, Catherine was twice as old as Korron.*

The door to study room 20 opened and closed gently, and a soft voice said, "I've got it, John. Found it right away."

John Fogolin's mood lifted measurably. One good thing — one very good thing — about this project was that Linda Sandness was in his trio. Because of that, he was almost grateful to Sister Augustinetta for the assignment, for although Linda didn't know it yet, she was going to be his date for the spring ball in two months.

Linda had returned from the resource center, where she had gone to look up details about the Seven Years' War. Her one-third of the trio's problem read:

> *Three years after the end of the Seven Years' War, Hezekiah and Martha Beame sailed with their three daughters from Bristol, England, to Saint John, New Brunswick, and a new life in the New World.*
>
> *Within two months of landing in Saint John, after a dispute with local authorities, Hezekiah Beame took the family to Boston, then shortly afterward to Rhode Island, where they settled permanently.*

"Listen," Linda said. "This really helps."

She moved immediately to the table where John sat, and began to read aloud from the book she carried. "The Seven Years' War," she read, "was fought in Europe, North America and India, between France, Austria, Russia and Sweden on one side, and England and Prussia on the other. It started when Prussia invaded Saxony in 1756 and —"

"Prepare yourselves, ye great unwashed! I have cut the Gordian knot!"

The downside of the project had arrived. The number three member of their "investigative trio" was Porky Schnarrfeldt, whose single but unforgettable claim to distinction at Quail Run Academy was that he had torched a fart in the boys' change room in the sixth grade, so successfully that he'd been hospital-ized with second-degree burns. Moreover, his assistant in the act, Denny Walchuk, who was even more maladroit than Porky, had dropped the lit match into a wastebasket and started a fire that set off a smoke alarm, which in turn brought in the fire brigade and caused the entire school to be evacuated into a snowstorm.

Porky's venture was known ever after as the-Fart-that-Cleared-the-Academy, but, unfortunately for him and even more for his classmates, it had raised his profile to unofficial clown laureate, and there were times, like the present, when he was very hard to take.

His entrance had completely dissipated John's dreamy admi-ration of Linda's hair, and made him just a bit angry. "Where were you, anyway, Schnarrfeldt?" John barked. "We don't even know what your information is!"

"*Pax vobiscum*, faithful companions." Porky made a sign of blessing over the table. "Your dutiful complicitor has graced the triumvirate with this nubby tidbit." He spread his arms and cleared his throat, as John and Linda looked at each other in defeat. This was obviously a prepared speech.

"Hearken, peasants. I read. Ahem. The Treaty of Paris," Porky declaimed, holding an encyclopedia as though he were in a pul-pit, "signed in 1783, signaled the conclusion of the American Revolutionary War and recognized the United States as a nation." He had pronounced "conclusion" *CON*-clusion, and when he said *NAY*-shun, John and Linda leaped in together before Porky got into his plantation-owner persona.

"What's the *first* part? The stuff you got from Sister?" John hadn't intended to, but he'd outshouted Linda.

Porky was undeterred. "I am not finished, peasant. You should also know that Rhode Island renounced allegiance to Great Britain in 1776, and that it signed the Constitution in 1790 and —"

"We know all that, Clarence," Linda said in a soft voice, using

Porky's real name. It had an instant effect. "What we need," she continued, "is your part of the trio information."

"I... yeah," Porky said. "Okay... uh... here."

He read:

> *When they landed at Saint John, Korron Beame was half as old as Magdalene had been when the Seven Years' War began.*

"That's all?" Linda asked.

"Yup." Porky nodded.

John's face broke into a huge grin. "You know," he said, I think it's enough!"

His smile broadened. Sister Augustinetta had overestimated how long it would take for them to get the answer, especially since it wasn't due till tomorrow morning. Now, if he could just find a way to get rid of Porky...

What is the answer to the problem Sister Augustinetta has given John, Linda and Porky?

34

Nothing Wrong with Helena, Montana

AS FAR AS STEVE FLECK was concerned, the one — the *only* — drawback to working here in Helena, Montana, was far outweighed by all the advantages. The drawback was that he never got to use his German, or his French, or his command of two Hungarian dialects. Nor was this considerable linguistic accomplishment recognized in his salary, or as a valuable asset in his department. Quite the opposite. Foreign languages, even here at the airport, only raised eyebrows. Just last month when Steve had taken a telephone call in the employees' lounge from his brother back in Uffenheim, and the two had nattered away, in German, about family gossip, his staff had gathered to stare in disbelief.

Still, Steve had dismissed this minor disadvantage years ago. Helena, he acknowledged, might be a bit of a backwater in the great international scheme of things, but being head of airport security here was a sight easier on the nerves than the same job in Frankfurt. He'd never gotten used to the sight of soldiers there, walking about in pairs, machine guns held crossways in front of their bodies. Nominally, these soldiers were under his charge, but he knew their first obedience was to the military hierarchy. And no one ever listened to him when he argued that their presence tantalized rather than deterred terrorists.

Charles de Gaulle in Paris was no better. There were even more soldiers in this airport, so he'd resigned after only a few months. As for Heathrow, he hadn't even bothered to go to the interview after walking through the terminal that served flights to the Middle East.

No, Helena, Montana, was just fine. Still a few too many guns for Steve's liking, but most of them were slung behind the cabs of pickup trucks. And they were hunting rifles, not machine guns. To boot, they weren't allowed into the airport, not even into the parking lot. That one had been Steve's most unpopular decree since becoming head of airport security some six years ago, but even that had faded as an issue when everyone got used to it.

In fact, Helena could well be the only airport in his considerable experience, Steve thought as he got to his feet to leave the office, where he could do precisely what he was doing right now and not feel guilty. That was to walk out while the fax machine — the one hooked into Immigration Security in Washington — was pushing out an incoming message. Messages to Helena never amounted to a pinch.

Besides, Steve was about to enjoy one of the pluses that had recently developed in this job. Two months ago he'd hired Meike Verwij to fill a vacancy in the floor staff. Not only was he able to use his smattering of Dutch now, but he also had designs on this attractive young lady, which she seemed to welcome. Meike had just buzzed him from the luggage area; the fax could wait.

The timing is perfect, he thought as he started down the wide staircase to the main floor. He could see Meike standing by the security barrier of the luggage area, and he knew that in five minutes she was due to have a break.

The anticipation faded, though, as he got closer. Meike had an anxious look on her face. And on the face of the man beside her was a look that, if anything, was ominous — and angry. He was expensively dressed and carefully manicured, his whole image pronounced by a head of elegant silver hair. He was being detained, and his aristocratic bearing made this affront to his dignity appear all the more ignominious.

There was no question of his stomping off, for behind him and Meike towered Jimmy Whitecloud, Meike's floor partner. Jimmy was reputed to be the biggest security guard in the business. Steve had to admit he'd never seen one bigger anywhere.

He put on his public-relations expression and walked toward them, but Meike darted forward and pulled him aside. She was apologetic.

"You said always to call you if we were suspicious, no matter what!" She was breathing very quickly and looking at Steve for confirmation.

He nodded, but his PR expression had now turned to a frown.

"And —" Meike was breathing even faster "— I hope I didn't do anything wrong here, but... see his luggage?"

Without being obvious, Steve shifted slightly to take in the two suitcases at the feet of the angry man. They were, like the man's clothes, top of the line and, while certainly not battered, seemed to be very much used. They'd seen travel — one of them in particular — with stickers, advertising such exotic locales as Jakarta, Dubai, Valparaiso and Buenos Aires.

Steve nodded again. He'd prepared a little Dutch expression on the way down, but somehow it didn't seem even remotely appropriate at the moment. That didn't matter; Meike wasn't interested in chitchat right now.

"You know how we're supposed to make people show their luggage ticket?" she said. "You know, match the ticket against the tag on the luggage?"

It was another one of the changes Steve had introduced. Most travelers were actually grateful. It precluded a lot of mixups.

"Yes, of course." He had spoken for the first time.

"Well, the man there — he couldn't find his. Oh, he did eventually. Had to go through all his pockets. His passport's Czechoslovakian. It must have a hundred stamps on it."

Steve was alarmed. "You surely didn't take his passport, did you? We're not authorized —"

"No, no. But what I do have is this."

For the first time Steve noticed the piece of paper in Meike's hand.

"You said if there's anything suspicious, we detain the person and call you, right?" Meike was breathing more comfortably now.

Again Steve just nodded. In spite of himself he was feeling a bit uneasy. There were times when he felt he overdid things. He knew that there were some on the airport board who thought so. However, after all those years in European airports — well, he just couldn't help it.

"So what is it you have?" he asked, reaching for the paper.

"His itinerary." Meike held it out, but he didn't take it from her. He could read it easily.

"He gave it to me to hold while he went through his pockets. His glasses, too, and the passport. That's before he got mad. It has to be an itinerary," Meike said. "See, the first date is yesterday. It shows a Pan Am flight to Chicago, then…" She put her finger on the second line. "Holiday Inn, 1-800-525-2242."

Steve could see the neat block lettering. The second date was today's, August 16, and it listed Northwest Airlines to Helena, Montana, then Best Western 1-800-528-1234. Tomorrow's was Northwest again, and it showed Calgary, Alberta: Hilton 1-800-268-9275. Then for August 18, Air Canada to Toronto, Ontario, Relax Inn 1-800-661-9563. The last was 19 August, United Airlines to Albany, New York: Howard Johnson 1-800-654-2000. Then at the bottom was a line, "Always call between 5:00 P.M. and 8:00 P.M. EST."

Steve looked at the man standing with his luggage under the shadow of Jimmy Whitecloud. Then he looked directly at Meike. "I wonder... Naw, it couldn't be. It's never in six years... I... Go stand with Jimmy. I'll be right back."

Taking the stairs two at a time, Steve dashed for his office and burst through the door. The fax was quiet now, but a two-page message dangled from the feeder gap. He tore it off.

"Level Two Alert," it said. "Detain for immigration authorities or local FBI." Then it went on to describe the suspected illegal entry into North America of Gert Neustadt, a.k.a Anton Dobrany, alleged 2IC of ODESSA. A second paragraph gave a brief summary of the man's alleged war crimes and a listing of procedures for contacting Immigration.

The second page had a computerized composite of Gert Neustadt's face. The fax, of course, couldn't illustrate silver hair, but the rest of the resemblance was unmistakable.

As he strode out the door, Steve felt a tingle of satisfaction at the realization he was going to be able to use his German, and this time the stares would be respectful ones. But what really gave him a charge was that he now had a very good reason to take Meike Varwij out to dinner!

No, there was surely nothing wrong at all with Helena, Montana. Nothing at all.

Obviously Meike found something suspicious about the silver-haired man that caused her to report to Steve Fleck. Exactly what was it?

SOLUTIONS

1
A Clean Place to Make
an End of It

One of the very clear pieces of evidence is that the body has been dead for some time. The odor makes that certain, so it is quite likely that, as the coroner says, the victim has been dead for forty to fifty hours.

Therefore, if the woman backed the car into the garage that long ago, and left the motor running until she died, the car would have run out of fuel, and the battery would have been drained to powerlessness owing to the fact that the ignition was left on. Yet Bob was able to lower one of the windows by simply ticking the switch. He suspects that this car may not be the place where the person died.

2
Chasing the Bank Robbers

The cars are very similar, and Kay has willed herself not to attend to details like license numbers because she's on vacation. So there's probably nothing in the appearance of the cars to influence her choice.

It's possible that the robbers used two identical cars and one then became a decoy in the subdivision, but the chasing policeman didn't mention that. And there's still only one patrol car to follow two possible suspects.

However, the first car had its signal light going. That fact, at a T intersection that is apparently blind, would suggest the driver has some idea where he or she is going, or at the very least knows the T intersection is there. Since the officer in the chase car has indicated that the robbers are local, it's probable that Kay MacDuffee will therefore recommend following the first car to the left.

3
The Power of Chance

In all likelihood, Walter "Whispering" Hope has impaired hearing. He speaks very loudly, which is typical of people with diminished hearing capacity. Still, this may just be habit from trying to communicate on construction sites. The clincher is seeing Hope at work on a backhoe without hearing protection. It's very likely he has hearing damage if that's the way he works.

There is another element that may also prove to be pertinent. Whether Tom knows it or not (he'll certainly discover it if he looks into Walter Hope) on most construction sites the workers wear yellow hard hats and the bosses wear white ones. If Hope is a bossman, he's likely been around these noisy places for some time.

If it's going to be Hope's testimony that he overheard the defendants trying to deal goods on the patio of a bar, which itself is not an acoustically ideal location, there is good reason to suspect his credibility as a witness.

4
On Flight 701 from Hong Kong

Ralph Ransom has quite correctly found several of both men's actions suspicious, although they would be quite ordinary and everyday if the men weren't the subjects of a tip. There's no reason why Huan Lee, for example, should not make a telephone call from the lobby before going to his room. It's done all the time, and it's hardly suspicious. Also, the fact that the man has little luggage may well indicate his experience as a traveler. Similarly, what's wrong with Won Lee buying chocolate bars? Or what's suspicious about being hyper? Lots of people are, whatever their race or color or sex or...

The fact that both men are named Lee is a coincidence that should not raise any eyebrows. It's a very common result when a Chinese name is translated into English: a Smith or Jones equivalent.

But Ralph has picked up a discrepancy. Won Lee's passport does not show any trips to North America, and he told Turpin it was his first visit. Yet this hyper man bought Mars bars in seconds — literally "pumps out the change" according to Iggie Kavanagh. Someone who has never been to Canada will not be familiar enough with the coinage to do that. Canadian nickels, dimes, quarters — not to mention the loonie — are different from the coinage in Hong Kong. A stranger would have to take longer than Won Lee did to identify the coins needed to buy a thing "in seconds."

Anyone who has ever been in a foreign country for the first time knows that getting used to the money is one of the most awkward adjustments. Mr. Won Lee is not exactly what he purports to be.

5
Trying to Find Headquarters

The group is supposed to go to St-Aubert. Whether Montgomery's headquarters is still there, or even if it ever got there, is not Doug's concern, since he and his little squad aren't aware of what is going on around them beyond the awareness of combat.

Fortunately the road sign to St-Aubert is still attached to the post, even if it's pointing into the ground. So is the sign pointing to Bayeux, from which they have been traveling. For Doug, it was a reasonably simple procedure to mentally position the sign with the Bayeux piece pointing back along the road they have been traveling, then follow the sign to St-Aubert.

6
The Case of the Disappearing Credit Card

Julie Iseler has some advantages in this situation. One is that when she and Tammy Hayward deal with the Saint twins, the boys can be distinguished by their respective double and single crowns — although that's only useful if the top backs of their heads can be seen. Another advantage is that her experience as a hair stylist has made her more than usually adept in the physics of mirrors.

But this is not to take away from her powers of logical deduction.

While she was talking to Mrs. Saint, Julie saw one of the boys carefully decorating a tattoo with red felt marker. She also noted that the other twin had already completed his in a similar fashion. From the incident of the pinch, the previous spring, she knows that Paul is left-handed. Thus Paul's tattoo must be on the crook of his right arm and Peter's tattoo on the crook of his left.

With the redecorating in Hair Apparent, Julie can only see the cash and waiting areas via two mirrors when she's at her chair (where indeed she was, attending to George, when the telephone rang and she saw the VISA card being taken.) Under the old decoration system, she'd have looked into only one mirror to see the waiting and cash areas. She realizes that in that situation, every image is reversed. (Right arms appear left and vice versa). But in the new system, the second mirror — the one on the side wall — re-reverses the image, so that in the second mirror a right arm would actually appear as a right (and left as left).

To conclude that Paul has taken the credit card, she must have seen a right arm with a tattoo on it reflected in the second mirror. (By the same token, had she seen a left arm with a tattoo, she'd have concluded it was Peter.)

7
A Badly Planned Saturday?

Taken together, there are pieces of circumstantial evidence that might nudge Jeff Baldwin and others into being suspicious. Especially if it can be determined that Dan Turner and Jeannie Burnside have a relationship that is more than just friendly. Most especially if such a relationship existed before the Saturday trip.

It was Jeannie who packed the food, after all, and she whose snowmobile did not have a spare drive belt.

There's only the word of these two survivors, too, for what happened.

Jeff has twigged to a discrepancy between their story and what he has seen in his follow-up visit. Turner said they had used Mark Burnside's saw to cut trees for a shelter. And there is indeed a shelter made of pine trees. Jeff photographed it. And the trees had been cut for some time — several months at least, for the needles were dead — but not long enough for them to have fallen off. The real matter, however, is the stumps. The one Jeff was sitting against was only as tall as his ear, about the height of an adult's torso and head. So were all the others. Yet when these trees were supposedly cut, the freshly fallen snow was as deep as Dan Turner's height, and it had fallen on top of what was already a record winter fall. The stumps of trees cut at that point would be much taller than the height of an adult torso and head.

Why were the stumps short then, almost normal? Had someone cut them in advance late last fall? Or first thing this spring? And if so, why? Why is the shelter part of the story patently untrue?

8
From *Sine Timore*
(The official newsletter of the National
Association of Security Services)

Since it was fairly certain that the cold-rolled steel parts were being carried out, first in duffle bags, then in the sealed cardboard boxes, it was a matter for Stephen of identifying which cardboard boxes they were concealed in.

Since the parts are heavy (cold-rolled steel is especially dense) they would add a considerable weight to what was supposed to be personal effects: clothing, for example. The obvious security method would have been to X-ray the boxes or simply heft them to find the heavy ones and open them. But that had already caused a strike. For reasons of labor peace, Stephen couldn't intervene in that way without very reasonable certainty of what he would find in a search.

By changing the "punch-out" procedures, Stephen devised a much subtler way of identifying boxes that were clearly heavier, and without touching them. Under his new system, the workers picked their individual time cards from the original wall rack, walked out the double doors to the lobby to stamp them and re-filed them in the rack there. In that process — at some point, if not all the time — the workers would have to carry their bread-box-sized cartons under one arm, resting on the hip. If the carton were heavy, the *other* arm would elevate; the body can't help it; the reaction is natural, and in the case of a very heavy weight, even necessary for balance.

Stephen waited till the third day. He was likely waiting until he was certain of a pattern.

(By the way, for Latin scholars: you were correct, *sine timore* means "without fear" or "without insecurity." Ablative case, of course.)

9
"Could Be the Biggest Thing Since Tutankhamen"

There are several questionable levels at which the rock climber's fraud might stumble, but not fall entirely. Isla de los Estados lies just off the eastern tip of Tierra del Fuego, and it *is* an unlikely spot to find a Stone Age tribe, principally because it's rather barren and subject to dreadful weather. Certainly there is no jungle there. Yet an inhospitable environment did not deter the aboriginal peoples in the very far northern latitudes. (And the tribe has established its quarters on the north of the mountain, away from prevailing winds at that latitude.)

Their food is mostly meat, which is logical given the climate, although one might be suspicious of the amount.

That there is no rear entrance/exit to the cave is cause for suspicion. Smoke from the fire might fill the cave. Still, the fire is at the entrance way; besides, early explorers in North America regularly reported the overwhelming smoke problem in the shelters of aboriginal peoples, so there's no reason for that to be an issue here, either.

What Thomas Arthur Jones probably noticed in many, if not all the photographs, was the neatness and the absence of garbage. Many of the shots revealed that areas surrounding the cave, and the cave itself, were very clean. Archaeologists look for garbage. The midden, or garbage heap, is a book in multiple volumes that tells them all about a people. This tribe, which had apparently been there awhile and planned to stay awhile, would by now have accumulated a goodly pile of refuse, and the rock climber, if he was "into archaeology in an amateur way," would have photographed it for sure. He'd have made a point of it. To Dr. Jones then, this is simply not the environment one could expect if the tribe were genuine.

10
A Report on Conditions at Scutari

Although the role of Bill Lacroix in this story is a fictional one, a real inspector during the Crimean War, like Bill, would have had much cause for frustration. That there was gross incompetence, not just in the field but in every facet of this war, has long been established by historians.

Many people know the war for the famous charge of Lord Cardigan's light brigade (which went in the wrong direction), or for the single most famous name from the conflict: Florence Nightingale, who did indeed cause dramatic changes in the administration and level of hygiene at the huge Barracks Hospital at Scutari. (Yet even Florence Nightingale's struggle went beyond the expected, for soon after her arrival in Scutari, she had to rule that she, and only she, could visit the wards after eight P.M., for some of her nurses had begun to take on duties with the men that had nothing to do with recuperative care!)

By reporting to the *Times* Fund (which raised £25,000 in 1854) Bill Lacroix would at least secure a willing ear. The "Russell chap" to whom the orderly refers — William Howard Russell, the first war correspondent ever* to actually write from the field — was vilified for his reports by the military, and called a "miserable scribbler" by the influential Prince Albert. No one in charge seemed to want to hear the truth about the Crimea, and it was only the courage of the editor at *The Times* that finally forced matters into the light.

By reporting to the *Times* Fund, Bill also would have had a clear chain of command, unlike the military in the Crimea. At the time, the British navy, responsible for moving the troops, had absolutely no connection with the army. Food and transport were actually the responsibility of the Department of the Treasury. The Medical Department reported to the Secretary for War (Sidney Herbert), while costs for the engagement were the responsibility of the Secretary for the Colonies!

In addition to all of the above, incredibly bad planning (Barracks Hospital was three hundred miles across the Black Sea from the Crimea and the fighting) and ill-disguised fraud were rife. It is an example of the latter that Bill Lacroix has noticed.

The "toff," the friend of Lord Raglan, in writing to Sidney Herbert, implies that Shed (or Ward) 14 has only sixteen patients, eight on each side. However, the beds in Shed 14 are arranged alternately, i.e., eight men lying with their feet toward the aisle and eight with their heads toward it, making sixteen on each side of the shed — thirty-two in all. When Bill stood at the side of the fusilier wounded with a bayonet, that soldier's head pointed to the outside. His head was right under the eave. The orderly, standing in the aisle at the bed behind Bill, was tapping the forehead of the soldier who had just died. When Bill asked the orderly to help pull beds farther into the aisle so the patients wouldn't be rained on, they pulled eight beds — every other one — in each row.

When the "toff" says that eight heads point out and eight pairs of feet point in, he's correct; but what he does not say is that there are eight heads and pairs of feet going the opposite way in each row, too. The intent is likely that Sidney Herbert will infer there is plenty of room in Shed 14, and since over-crowding was a major issue at Barracks Hospital, this report will surely mislead.

*The flamboyant Russell is often cited by trivia buffs as the *first* war correspondent. Although he was likely the first to report on-site truthfully, he was not the first correspondent. Media historians generally agree the first was Henry Crabb Robinson, hired by the *Times* in 1807 to report on the war against Napoleon in Central Europe. Robinson tended to use local newspapers as his source, rather than interviews or first-hand observation.

11
At the Scene of the Accident

There are two accounts of the accident here. Since the accounts are so widely different, at least one of them must be a fabrication. What Peterson missed is the time factor.

If the driver of the Corvette is telling the truth about where she has been, then the engine of her car will be cool to the touch. The Mercedes, of course, will be warm, but that's not the issue. If the Corvette is warm, then there is still a matter of working out who is telling the truth. But if it's cold, then clearly it was not on the road hitting a dog only a few minutes ago, as the Mercedes-Benz driver said.

12
The Midterm Exam:
Which Way Is Up?

The map seems to have picked up some printer's ink marks from the book in which it was stored for many years. That would account for the horizontal lines seen faintly over the H, and for the number 18, which appears in the bottom left-hand corner as the students view it on the screen. In this view (call it view 1) the treasured religious object is in the vertical shaft on the left. Now rotate the image 180 degrees (in your head or on paper). Call this view 2. In view 2, the treasured object is in the vertical shaft on the *right*. However, the number 18 is now in the upper right-hand corner, and has become the number 81.

Views 1 and 2 would be possible results if the map had been stored facing a left-hand page in the book. But that can't be. View 1 would mean that the number had rubbed off the page onto the map from the inside margin or bottom left-hand "gutter" (or call it the bottom of the right margin of the left-hand page if you prefer, or even the bottom right-hand corner). Books are not printed this way. Since medieval times, when monks were laboring away in their scriptoria, book pages have always been numbered in their upper or lower *outside* corners. Occasionally they will be numbered in the center of the page, top or bottom, but never in the inside margins or "gutters." (A very few reference books are rare exceptions to this.)

So, view 1 is not possible, or at best, highly improbable. View 2 is not possible because books are numbered with the even number on the left-hand page and odd on the right. If the map were facing the left-hand page in view 2, the number rubbing off would not be 81.

Therefore the map was stored facing a *right*-hand page.

Create view 3 by turning the page to view 2, then turning it over. Number 81, in this view, would again have rubbed off from the inside gutter: not very likely.

In view 4, which you get by rotating view 3 180 degrees, the number 81, an odd number, would have rubbed off from the bottom outside corner of the *right*-hand page — which is entirely possible and plausible. In fact, it is the only view that makes logical sense and must therefore be the correct one. In this view, the treasured object is in the left vertical shaft of the H, with the booby trap in the right.

Conceivably, Sean and MaryPat's students have a fifty-percent chance of guessing this, but the exam requires them to explain their reasoning. (Some students may reason that the number bled through the map from the other side, throwing off entirely the logic above. But that is not likely, for the text that appears only as vague lines on the H would then have been clearer, too. As well, thinner absorbent paper was not generally available until late in the nineteenth century.)

13
The Final Exam: Digging in the Right Place

The complications are several. For one thing, you don't know whether the treasured religious object is Salubrian or Egregian, so you may have to dig in both sites. Then, of course, you have to dig down the safe, *un*booby-trapped shaft in each case.

The key is first of all to find out in which country these shafts have been dug, and to do that you approach *either* of the two adults you see before you. It makes no difference which one you approach, if you ask the right question.

The question you ask is: "Are we standing, right now, in your country?" (or a variation that asks the same thing). You ask this because you can depend on Salubrians to be truthful and Egregians to prevaricate. Therefore, if you are standing in Salubria when you ask the question, a Salubrian will say "Yes" (the truth) and an Egregian will say "Yes" (a lie). On the other hand, if you are in Egregia, an Egregian will answer "No" to that question (a lie) and a Salubrian "No," as well (the truth). Therefore the answer "No" always means you're in Egregia; the answer "Yes" puts you in Salubria, no matter which of the two adults you ask and no matter what his or her nationality.

Armed with that information, you go back to your earlier research, from which you know that Salubrians perform all religious ceremonies facing south (and Egregians the opposite). If you get a "Yes" at one (or both) of the sites, then you put the setting sun on your right and make sure you are *facing* the shafts (south) before you dig. (If you passed the midterm exam, you'll dig down the shaft on the left.)

Should you find you're in Egregia, you'll put the setting sun on your left, and face the shafts before digging — the left one again.

14
A Double Assassination at "The Falls"

The two diplomats were of significantly different height. One was about the height of the sergeant, who is a head taller than Vince. The other was about Vince's height.

When Vince sat in the driver's seat of the car, waiting for clearance to tow it away, he adjusted the rearview mirror *down* so he could see out the back. Therefore it must have been adjusted for a taller person before: the taller of the two diplomats.

15
They Come in Threes, Don't They?

It isn't important to pin the date with exact precision here, only to realize the time is the late 1950s. At this time, telephone exchanges in North America — in fact, in most of the world — had names like *Walnut, Baker, Pennsylvania,* the first two letters of which were part of individual telephone numbers. Thus, Walnut 8-7425 (which today would be 928-7425) was usually written WA 8-7425. (And Pennsylvania 6-5000, was written PE 6-5000.)

It is R. David Sloan's telephone number that troubles Dale. Certainly his exchange would have had a name, but definitely not *Quaker.* That's because there was no letter *Q* on telephone dials. There is no *Q* today, either. Not on telephone dial wheels, and not on push-button phones (so being "too young" to solve this mystery is no excuse!).

Whatever Sloan's reason, he has given a phony number.

The precise date, incidentally, is 1958.

Ford Motor Company brought out two model years of its monumental flop, the Edsel: 1958 and 1959. Likely, the Dunns bought a 1958 Edsel (which would have come out in late 1957), since Mike refers to its purchase "last year."

The information about Castro makes the time 1958 instead of the other possibility, 1959, because it was in 1958 that Fidel Castro metamorphosed from gloriously welcomed liberator of Cuba (complete with a huge rally in New York's Central Park) into hated dictator (at least in the eyes of the U.S.). One of his first actions when he took over in 1958 was to nationalize most of the major industries, especially sugar.

16
Witness to a Hit-and-Run

The connection between the *black* Jimmy that Betty and her husband own, and the *blue* Jimmy that Betty describes as the hit-and-run vehicle, is at least as ominous as it is coincidental. Certainly Diane Van Hoof wants to talk to the husband, for Betty's story just doesn't wash.

The sun was in Diane's face as she sat in the café, so it was setting. (She'd just had a caribou burger from the luncheon menu, so it's not rising.) This makes the time of her meeting with Betty sometime after midday, likely early afternoon.

The time is winter, and Labrador, which ranges from approximately the 52nd parallel in the south to the 60th in the north, has very short days in winter. (January temperature range is minus 22 to minus 4 degrees Fahrenheit, or minus 20 to minus 30 degrees Celsius.)

If Betty has to get home from this meeting at the Two Seasons in order to set out a meal so that it will be ready for her husband when he gets home, it means that currently she's setting it out at a time when darkness prevails. If Betty, looking from the lit indoors to the dark outdoors, claims to have seen a *blue* Jimmy, there is reason for Diane to be doubtful.

It's also clear that the husband is working the day shift this week. This shift customarily ends around 3:00 or 4:00 P.M. (Next week he'll be on the swing shift, which is usually 3:00 or 4:00 P.M. to 11:00 P.M. or midnight; and he's not working the night shift right now.) This means he's driving home at approximately the time when the children have been dismissed from school and will be on the roads. And they would be on the roads, too. With enough snow to produce giant snowbanks on the airport runways, there's not going to be any sidewalk clearing. There's simply no place to put the snow!

Although Diane would not yet voice this suspicion, it's

possible that Betty's husband is engaging in a very hamhanded attempt at diverting attention in advance from a *black* Jimmy — just in case there is another witness. If the child was hit while Betty was setting out her husband's meal, the accident must have occurred at about the time when he was coming home.

17
The Plot at the Rockface

Trevor Hawkes needs the cooperation of his five fellow prisoners if his plan is going to work. However, he has reason to be positive in his outlook, especially since he is the only one who stands a chance of getting them safely down the mountains to Dubrovnik once they are on the other side — which is where they'll all want to be once Igor is dispatched.

There are two restrictions to Trevor's basket plan. One is that the royalists must never outnumber Nova's party. (He's counting on Nova, who is known to want to solve the Communist/royalist dispute, and who therefore would not be party to, or permit, any murdering of royalists if the opposite should occur and the royalists be outnumbered at any point in the escape process.) The other is that the basket needs two people going over and at least one coming back.

For simplicity's sake, let the Communist three be identified as T (for Trevor), N (for Nova) and C3. The three royalists are R1, R2 and R3.

a) T and R1 go across. R1 is left there and T brings the basket back.

b) R2 and R3 cross. A tricky stage since all three royalists are now on the other side and may well decide to take off. Trevor is counting on their not knowing where to go or — since they are farmers and a civil servant — *how*. This is mountain wilderness. R3 brings the basket back.

c) N and C3 cross. R2 returns with the basket.

d) T and R2 cross. T returns for R3.

Given the isolation of their work post and the fog that Trevor is counting on, the escape should succeed.

As a matter of historical interest:

The British Special Air Service, the SAS, is so carefully shrouded in mystery that many people believe (because of its famous success during the hostage incident at the Iranian Embassy in London) that it was formed only in recent years as an antiterrorist force. The SAS was established in the Western Desert in 1941, the brainchild of Lieutenant David Stirling, a man with some unorthodox ideas about how to defeat Rommel. By 1944-45, when this story is set, the SAS was thoroughly established as an elite, lethal, behind-the-lines commando organization.

The only slight anomaly in Trevor Hawkes's situation is that SAS agents usually work in pairs that link together in various numbers to form "operational squads." Trevor seems to be working alone.

18
Regina Versus Kirk

On the most obvious point — that Devon Kirk's wedding ring was at the murder scene — Bill Seeley will no doubt argue Kirk's explanation of why Thorvald Heintzmann had it. As well, it seems almost ludicrous that Kirk would leave such clearly incriminating evidence lying about. A moot point is that none of Kirk's fingerprints were found in the study, although the two men obviously saw quite a bit of each other. If an argument is made that Kirk was careful to wipe away all his prints, it would hardly be consistent to leave the ring behind.

That the murder weapon probably belongs to Kirk is not in dispute. John Ford will very likely suggest to the jury that the fact it was reported stolen on April 9 is at best a clumsy setup, in preparation for murder. However, Bill Seeley has a point to make in the nature of the wounds. If Kirk is a marksman who belongs to a gun club, surely he would be able to shoot more accurately at close range, as suggested by Dr. Quinn's description of the body's wounds. And quite likely a marksman would have needed only one shot.

A discrepancy arises in the testimony of Royal Orchard, which possibly neither Ford nor Seeley expected. Inspector Regan says that her prints were found in Thorvald Heintzmann's study — the only prints besides Heintzmann's own. Yet in answer to Ford's question about phoning the police, Royal Orchard says she never went into the study.

Finally, the matches from the Olde Thornhill Bar suggest that Kirk may have been in Heintzmann's study. The deceased may or may not have been a smoker, but Kirk is. And he was at this bar shortly before the murder. However, as Inspector Regan has described the book of matches, they were used by a right-handed person, for the ones removed from under the Ls had to be taken off by a righthander. (Try to get a leftie to take off matches from the right side of a match book!) Kirk must be left-handed if the umpire wouldn't let him pitch with his wedding ring on, so these aren't his matches. Heintzmann, on the other hand, given Inspector Regan's analysis of the attempt to write a message, seems to have been right-handed, and since he frequented the Olde Thornhill Bar, the matches may well have been ones that he used. He or Royal Orchard.

19
Danger at the Border

The Fewsters and the Mounts had the van breakdown by the head of a valley as they were heading north. Now the road ahead of them forks as it enters the valley.

As Juan Tomas re-emerges from the right fork (which he had gone up earlier) he points to his right in hitchhiker thumb style and announces that the choice should be the left fork, the one that runs north or *norte*. Therefore the right fork, where he has been, must be more or less easterly, or at least northeasterly, if not due east. In any case, he would have been walking into the rising sun that morning (they had breakfast at first light) either directly, or if the direction is more northeasterly, then with the sun to his right.

At his return, Juan Tomas reports seeing the sun reflect off the lenses of binoculars, suggesting possibly soldiers or bandits. Gene and Frank — Ann and Connie would surely have seen through it, too — pick up that he is lying. Juan Tomas pointed up the valley wall. That's the sun side, and to look down at the road a binocular user would have his or her back to the sun. There would be no reflection off the lenses.

Is Juan Tomas a setup man for whoever is up there? The party can't be sure. All they know is that he's lying, and given present conditions, they have good reason to suspect an ambush if they go the way Juan Tomas wants.

20
The Case of the Strange Hieroglyphs

Deirdre has detected a mirror pattern in the symbols they have seen. The first symbol is the numeral one (1), with the numeral in its proper form on the right, and its mirror image on the left. At Karmo's suggestion, they took the tunnel to the right. They did the same thing at the second archway, where the numeral two (2) appeared (on the right, with its image mirrored to the left). Now at the third archway, they have seen the numeral three (3), with its mirror image on the left.

Each time they have taken the right fork, or the side on which the true or sponsoring image of the double pattern occurs. Deirdre believes that if they take the right tunnel again at the third arch, they will come to a fourth arch with this symbol over it, giving the numeral four (4) with its mirror image. *This time* they will take the left tunnel.

Whether the Crusaders are responsible for the tunnels and the symbols could well be the subject of lengthy debate. The numerals are Arabic, and Arabic numerals were introduced into Europe at the beginning of the thirteenth century (by Leonardo Pisano Fibonacci — if you want to impress your friends). In

1228, the aggressive and very successful Frederick II, king of Germany, king of Sicily, king of Jerusalem, launched the Sixth Crusade.

Frederick was certainly in Acre, and he was likely to have been a leader in the use of the Arabic numeral system, for he was a patron of art and science. More proof than that would be needed to attribute the tunnels and the symbols to him, but Deirdre can enjoy the satisfaction of knowing that it's highly unlikely they are Phoenician, or even remotely connected to that culture.

Deirdre's use of "off" to indicate direction is from cricket. It means "on the same side of the field as the batsman's bat." If Karmo's flashlight (his electric torch) is in his right hand, his "off" side is then his right side (thereby making the left his "near" side).

21
The Fuchsia Track Suit Kidnapping

It could well be that the Potishes are setting things up for Geoff. Mrs. Potish claims to be a bird watcher, a sufficiently serious bird watcher to be recording her sightings. It's fairly difficult to accomplish that in a fuchsia track suit that doesn't appear to have encountered dirt or perspiration. Bird watching, *true* bird watching, often involves a lot of crawling through awkward spots in both bush and field.

By itself that's not much, but it does go along with the manicured hands — hardly the style of an avid bird watcher. Not that bird watchers don't have manicures. However, they do get *out* to do much of their watching. Some of it may be done from chairs in front of windows, especially in the winter, but this is certainly not winter, if the flag person in the tank top and denim shorts is any indication.

Still, the most important clue to Geoff comes from the dust on the windowsill. It is in a neat layer. If Stasia Potish had spent some considerable time in the chair, at the window with the binoculars, it is reasonable to expect the dust on the sill to be disturbed or smudged. Whatever she was doing for some time this morning, it was likely not sitting in front of the window with binoculars, looking for a European finch.

22
An Almost Perfect Spot

Cecile King is already nervous because of her vague certainty that she saw MaryClare McInerney in Azure that morning, so she is understandably alert. The fact that she did not suspect anyone in the "Cobbleton Pin Busters" crowd suggests how clever that cover was for the man with the slouching gait. How he managed to draw attention to himself — which both Cecile and Dorothy picked up in time — was by failing to act like a tourist despite his very obvious tourist cover.

A real tourist would not have walked so purposefully past The Espadrille, and surely the glassblower would have merited a look. Also, tourists don't usually go directly into a difficult-to-see delicatessen — especially with the distractions of Azure — unless they already know where they are going.

Cecile and Dorothy may not know who the man is or what he is doing, but in their business, all they really need to know is that this very obvious tourist is probably not a tourist at all. Whatever he is, they don't want him near their exchange.

23
The Interrupted Patrol

Chief Gary Ellesmere has reason to be cautious. He's alone in an isolated area with only the word of an agitated man that a woman has been hurt or killed in the kitchen of the farmhouse. Extreme prudence would dictate that he wait for backup rather than go in alone, but Gary feels he has the perpetrator in front of him. It could be he is suspicious of the man for saying he was going back to the house for a drink of water. Why wouldn't he drink from the Tap or the Creek, since they're so close? Still, when the man said "Just past the creek," he might have simply meant "the creek" and not "the Creek."

More likely, Gary is uneasy about the man's alibi. He said he had been checking fences for the previous half hour, and pointed out the field. Gary could see the field had not been grazed for some time. Because the weather has been dry and hot, the vegetation, especially thistles and burdocks and similar weeds that thrive along fences, would be tall and hard and prickly. No one who knows he is going to walk the perimeter to check the fence would ever wear shorts. If the man's wife has been murdered, Gary will want a better explanation of his whereabouts before he went back to the house and discovered the body.

24
The View from the Second-floor Promenade

Despite the attention Daisy attracted, the newspapers she was piling made it quite plain that a prisoner from the nearby penitentiary was on the loose. Not just an everyday prisoner, either, but someone who had apparently killed, and who had been in jail a long time.

Prisoners don't open doors. Doors are opened for them, either electronically or manually by guards. Over time, prisoners become habituated to standing in front of doors, waiting for them to open — like the man in the green jacket.

25
Death in the Bide-a-Wee Motel

Dolores Dexel feels that the scene has been tampered with and that the person(s) who did it may still be around. Her deductions are based on the circumstances of the Gideon Bible. From where she stood at the victim's feet (she could read the brand name on his new heels) she was looking along the body and out to the doorway. And from that perspective she could see the victim's left hand (the wedding ring) grasping the edge of the book, with the palm over the page. On the uncovered page, Dolores could see a double column of text top to bottom.

Miss Duvet reported that in her "picture," she could see the Bible open to "The Gospel according to Matthew." Since she did not go into the room, Miss Duvet must have read that from the hallway or at best from the doorway. In this case, with the poor lighting, the only type large enough to actually read would have been the type from a title page.

A title page always appears on the *recto* (right-hand) side of a book. That's the way a book is laid out for printing. For an important or main title, or one indicating a major change in contents, it would be exceedingly rare to find it on the left or *verso* page. Matthew is the first of the four gospels of the New Testament — a major change in contents — and a Bible with the title page to the Matthew gospel on the left would be an extremely unusual one.

What all this means is that if Dolores saw a double column of text top to bottom on the exposed page when she was in the motel room with the body, then the title page (on the recto or right-hand side) is covered by the victim's hand. And the book, in that case, is turned *toward* the doorway. When Miss Duvet said she read "Gospel according to Matthew" upside down, it means the book was turned *away* from the doorway at the time. The recto side, the one with the title, would have been the uncovered page if this were the case.

Dolores is taking the position that Miss Duvet is telling the truth. There's no reason for her to have falsely added the bit about reading the title page upside down.

Finally, Dolores's deductions have determined that if someone moved the Bible, it must have happened fairly soon after the killing, because when she came to the scene the blood had framed the book neatly. It had flowed around after the book was moved; there would have been smudging otherwise. (It also means that Miss Duvet came upon the scene very shortly after the man was killed, which is why Dolores would like to know more about the time when she called.)

26
Bailing Out the Navy
— for a Price

Someone with Bob Ashby's long experience in industrial design, and with his innate distrust of Thurman Elliott, Jr., might be able to determine, without pen and paper, why the proposal from Ashburn Engineering is something of a "sting" of the navy. The rest of us will be better off with a diagram to help us visualize.

The broken chains are in pieces of three links each, and

there are twenty of these pieces. The navy wants all these pieces restored to four chains of equal length, so five of the broken pieces will be needed for each. One chain, therefore, would look like this prior to being restored.

Thurman Elliott's proposal, at $10,000 per cut-and-weld, would cost $40,000 for each chain. Times four such chains would make his proposed total of $160,000.

Reasonable enough. But Bob Ashby knows there is a less expensive way to do it, even if Thurm Elliott's high cut-and-weld rate is used. Bob's idea is to open all three links in *one* of the pieces, and use them to unite the remaining four pieces. This system requires only *three* cuts-and-welds per chain. At $10,000 per, that's $30,000 per chain. Times four chains is $120,000.

27
The Case of the Missing .38 Smith and Wesson

It is indeed conceivable that someone could have found a gun in a puddle created by construction. And, as Gary observes, the Smith and Wesson .38 is a fairly common weapon. But the potential suspect's story is flawed from two perspectives:

For one thing, the puddles created by road construction, or any construction for that matter, are rarely filled with clean or even translucent water. Usually it's very dirty, and it would be difficult for anyone to see a gun lying in it (unless he already knew it was there). For another — and this is probably the one that confirms Gary Westlake's suspicions — the puddle is quite likely to be ice-covered, frozen over.

Whoever last used Car 9119 had the fan rear defrost on. A toque, nonregulation, but sometimes used by the highway patrol, was lying on the front seat. The only reason to wear one would be to keep warm. Finally, Gary is wearing gloves. Taken together, the three clues should be sufficient to point to cold winter weather, and ice on still water.

28
On the Trail of the Stolen Horses

Marv Chantler was unable to see the hoofprints he was looking for on the trail to which the farm woman had directed him. That in itself is not enough to warrant serious suspicion. He was looking for the unshod right foreleg of the piebald mare, but he had, after all, lost the trail even before coming to the farm itself. It is entirely possible that the piebald, and the other two horses, have been taken up this trail but that their tracks are indistinguishable and Marv simply can't detect them.

What distresses Marv is the woman's implication that he can't see the prints he's looking for because rain has altered them. When Marv went up the trail this morning, he dismounted near the two alder stumps. There, following the tracks of the wolf or dog, he noticed a varmint hole covered by dusty cobwebs. The dust would have come partly from the breezes and partly — probably mostly — from the surface of the trail being stirred up by horses' hooves. Had sufficient rain fallen since the horses went up there, a couple of days or so ago, to alter or obliterate their tracks, it would also have drenched the cobwebs and washed the dust off, or quite likely have destroyed the cobwebs.

The farm woman acknowledged seeing three horses, two of which fitted the description of the stolen ones, so she knows what Marv is asking about. What he would like to know now is why she sent him up the wrong trail.

29
The Royal Blue Escort

Harvey and Vin are staked out on a one-way street. If Keffer is so obsessed with blending in and not being noticed, one of the elementary strategies he would surely follow is to avoid attracting attention with simpleminded traffic violations such as going the wrong way up a one-way street, as the driver of the blue Escort did.

By the same token, Harvey and Vin are on a stakeout and, in turn, don't want to attract attention, by "coming down," as Harvey put it, on someone unless they're sure of their mark. The driver of the Escort is so unlikely a suspect, because he drove the wrong way on Robb Road, that Vin and Harvey reached the same conclusion together, without discussion, and decided against pursuit or detention.

The two agents are in England, obviously; in Wythenshawe, a suburb of the city of Manchester. Traffic, as everyone knows, flows on the left side of the road; vehicles are operated from the front right seat. Vin is in the driver's seat. Harvey sits opposite. Because Harvey bumped his elbow on the parking meter, they are parked on the left side of Robb Road (as is customary). Harvey can see the front of No Parking signs all the way down

Robb Road, on the other side. The signs are thus facing their Rover. That means the signs are intended to be read by traffic moving along Robb Road in the same direction Harvey and Vin are facing. If two-way traffic were allowed, the signs would face the other way.

30
An Unlikely Visitor — or Two

Before Gutenberg and the popular use of movable type, most books of the medieval period were handwritten and beautifully decorated on *vellum*, parchment made of the skins of calves and lambs. But printers use paper, which is less suitable for gold decoration and painting. It may be reasonable to assume that the Book of Hours Miles N. Miles has brought to Struan is indeed from medieval Europe. (Struan himself, truly sensitive to the chemical effect of fingertips on the gold decoration, feels the text with the back of his hand.) The clue to the book's age, however, is in a phrase that is commonly known and equally commonly, and wrongly, attributed to the Bible.

"Cleanliness is next to godliness" is an admonition from the pen of John Wesley, the eighteenth-century British clergyman acknowledged as the founder of Methodism. (It's from one of Wesley's sermons, entitled "On Dress," and is based on a passage from the *New* Testament.) Thus the phrase, which Struan says is in poor Latin in any case, could not have been copied out by a medieval scribe in a monastery.

The Bible, incidentally, is wrongly attributed as the source for a number of popular sayings: "Fools rush in where angels fear to tread," for example, is from Alexander Pope's *Essay on Criticism*, written in 1711. "Spare the rod and spoil the child" is from English poet Samuel Butler's *Hudibras*, written in

1664. And the Bible itself gets altered. The famous "Pride goeth before a fall" is actually "Pride goeth before destruction, and an haughty spirit before a fall" (from *Proverbs*).

Given all this, and the other pressures on Miles N. Miles, it's understandable that he (they?) would seek advice.

31
The Mission in the Clearing

In the days before blood packs and refrigerated plasma supplies, or in conditions where these things were unavailable, it was not unusual to transfuse directly from one person to another in an emergency. Since Haight-Windsor is O-negative, the surviving priest will be able to receive his blood, because O-negative is a universal donor, as Ron Forrester says. (Other factors of course, would be taken into account in a modern hospital, but that's not where this is happening!)

Throckton believes that with enough blood, Haight-Windsor's and Ron's — if it's the right type — he can keep the priest alive until they get to the airstrip. The question is this: is the priest A-positive like Ron?

Using the following reasoning, he is, and given the emergency and the fact that he is *in extremis*, anyway, it's the best they have. Of the two priests who were bound together, the one on the left is somewhat unkempt and disheveled. He is the one who is alive (his Roman collar was dirty) and also the one whose right shoe is scuffed at the heel from top to bottom. That's the kind of scuff a right shoe gets if it is worn by a vehicle driver. The heel wears from the rotation at the accelerator. This particular priest must be the one who drives the mission's pickup truck then, and it must be his blood type disk (A+) on the ring with the ignition key.

32
Trespassing on the MBA Property

The solution here has much to do with the season, the terrain, the vegetation and the time sequence. Whether or not one needs the precision of Ron Minaker's apparent knowledge of geology, it is clear that the place where the helmet was allegedly found is in a hilly area, with many rises and hollows.

Jack Atkin, who seems to be in better shape for walking than his two friends, has arrived at the spot earlier than they, and has had time to look down from the top of a knoll into the hollow on the MBA property where the helmet is supposed to have been found. At this point, he has analyzed the time sequence and the seasonal factor.

If Indian summer has come and gone, this is October, possibly September or November, but no earlier or later. (Even without knowing when Indian summer arrives — and it doesn't always — it's still obvious that this is late autumn, for the leaves have gone and it's not yet winter.) The ATV accident must have occurred about July, or certainly in the summer. That's when the helmet, worn or not, would have come off there, if indeed the accident occurred there.

If Sasha Dahlman's elder brother and two friends reported seeing it from the top of the hill *yesterday*, and if the last of the leaves had been blown off the mature maple, ash and oak trees just under a week before, the fact is they couldn't have seen it as reported. In a treed area, with knolls and hollows, the wind will blow the dried leaves into the hollows, even filling them if there are enough trees. The helmet, deposited in the summer, would have been well covered by yesterday afternoon, so Jack has found an effective counter to use before the jury — if it comes to that.

33
When History Becomes Math

The Seven Years' War began in 1756, according to information Linda found in the resource center. If, as her part of the trio's information says, the Beame family went to the New World three years after the end of that war, they would have sailed from Bristol to Saint John in 1766. (1756 + 7 + 3 = 1766) During the voyage, Magdalene celebrated her eighteenth birthday, according to John's information. Therefore, if she married in Pawtucket at the age of twenty-two and had her firstborn two years later, Magdalene's firstborn would have arrived in 1772. (18 in 1766; 22 in 1770; baby born in 1772).

When the Seven Years' War began, Magdalene would have been eight years old. According to Porky's information, when the family landed in Saint John (in 1766) Korron was half as old as Magdalene had been at the beginning of the Seven Years' War. Therefore, Korron was four years old in 1766. She'd have been twenty-two in 1784 (1766 + 18) and her firstborn would then have seen the light for the first time in 1786.

From the information John has, Catherine was eight years old in 1766 (twice as old as Korron). She'd have married in Pawtucket then, in 1780, and given birth to her first in 1782.

From this point it becomes a matter of the trio's notion of what constitutes citizenship. Porky makes clear that Rhode Island, where all three married and had their firstborn, renounced allegiance to Great Britain in 1776. Quite likely, Magdalene's firstborn (1774) was born a British citizen. Korron's quite likely can be seen as an American citizen, since he or she was born after the Treaty of Paris in 1783.

Only the citizenship of Catherine's baby is debatable, since it was born after the beginning of the American Revolution (while Britain still regarded Rhode Island as its colony) but before 1783 when Britain recognized the U.S. as a nation. Quite likely, this is a debate John Fogolin would prefer to take up in private with Linda Sandness, assuming he can find something for Porky Schnarrfeldt to do elsewhere!

34
Nothing Wrong with
Helena, Montana

Gert Neustadt (if indeed this is Gert Neustadt) is presenting the image of being a well-traveled individual, as the heavily stamped passport and the luggage with its stickers would suggest. An experienced traveler would not be likely to prepare an itinerary that lists the hotels where he is staying, using 800 telephone numbers. Anyone trying to contact him between 5:00 and 8:00 P.M., EST, would have a very difficult time doing so, because these are central reservation numbers for the hotel chain. He couldn't be reached at a specific hotel through an 800 number.

Not a big deal, but Meike has twigged to a discrepancy between the image and the reality and is simply following Steve's dictate that anything remotely suspicious gets reported. The fact that a general announcement about Neustadt has arrived by fax at just this moment is purely coincidence, but, then, this may show that the good guys do win sometimes.

Gert Neustadt, if he is second in command of ODESSA, is an officer in an organization of interesting, probably unsavory, characters. ODESSA is the "Organization der Ehemalige SS Angehöriger" — the Organization of Former Members of the SS.

Incidentally, some readers of *Nothing Wrong with Helena, Montana*, may put two and two together and come up with five by assuming that Meike may actually have recognized Gert Neustadt, for her name is quite clearly European. However, the fax machine, the computerized image, etc., put the time frame pretty much in the present. Since Meike is described as a "young lady," she would have been too young to have known Neustadt during or even after the Second World War.